The Voice from the
Mendelsohns' Maple

The Voice from the Mendelsohns' Maple

Mary C. Ryan

Illustrated by
IRENA ROMAN

LITTLE, BROWN AND COMPANY
Boston · Toronto · London

First edition

The characters and events portrayed in this book are
fictitious. Any similarity to real persons, living or dead, is
coincidental and not intended by the author.

Library of Congress Cataloging-in-Publication Data

Ryan, Mary C.
   The voice from the Mendelsohns' maple / Mary C.
Ryan. — 1st ed.
     p.   cm.
   Summary: Penny's expectations of a long boring
summer are exploded when she meets an elderly,
practically naked, woman in a tree and soon finds herself
embroiled in a mystery involving the Beacon Manor
Senior Citizen Residence.
   ISBN 0-316-76360-8
   [1. Old age — Fiction. 2. Mystery and detective
stories. 3. Humorous stories.] I. Title.
PZ7.R9545Lad 1989
[Fic] — dc19   89-31569
                                          CIP
                                          AC

10 9 8 7 6 5 4 3 2 1

HAD

Published simultaneously in Canada
by Little, Brown & Company (Canada) Limited
PRINTED IN THE UNITED STATES OF AMERICA

To
MARION SEIPPEL MOORE,
who gave me life, love, and
the best Toll House cookies ever,

and to
MARY GLADYS STAEBELL RYAN,
a fellow writer and good friend.

The Voice from the
Mendelsohns' Maple

1

I don't usually go around talking to trees, but after all, I *was* brought up to be polite, so when the Mendelsohns' maple spoke to me that day in July, I guess my reaction was spontaneous.

(SPONTANEOUS: *adjective:* natural or instinctive. That's one of Miss Cooper's big words — the kind she's always suggesting I look up and then use so I'll improve my vocabulary. Well, here I am using them. I wonder, though, if she'd approve of my telling this story, because we did agree to forget the whole thing. But I figured I might have to come up with something creative for Language Arts class someday, and it wouldn't hurt to be prepared. Nobody would ever suspect it really happened.)

Anyway, what made my response to the tree even more *spontaneous* was what it said.

The word was "*Help!*"

Tucker Street, basking in the late-afternoon sun,

was nearly deserted. A few houses down, a couple of little girls were wheeling a toy grocery cart along the sidewalk and picking stones and stuff up off the ground, pretending they were in a supermarket, I suppose.

It was about five-thirty. I'd spent the entire day baby-sitting the Lawler twins, who were seven and had quite a way to go before they turned into anything even resembling adults.

Mrs. Lawler had barely left the house that morning when Ronnie dumped a canister of flour all over the kitchen floor, so that it looked like a blizzard had hit the place. I swept up the mess as best I could and in the process got something under my contact lens. The twins had already disappeared outside. I thought I'd better catch them before they destroyed the entire neighborhood, so I popped out my lens, stuck it in a glass of water to keep it wet, and followed.

The two of them were busily snapping off flower buds and whizzing them at each other. Just then a bee stung Rory. He screamed so loud that nosy Mrs. McGruder from across the street came charging over to see who I was murdering.

"Put some mud on it," she suggested.

Ronnie picked up on that right away and turned on the hose. Maybe he thought he was aiming it someplace else (and maybe he didn't), but the water caught Mrs. McGruder smack in the face. By the time I got it shut off, she'd gone sputtering back home and the

4

boys were having a great time making mud pies. They were already too dirty to worry about, so I let them play for a while and then took them inside to clean up. Before I could even think, one of them (they're identical, and I wasn't sure which) picked up the glass of water from the counter and drank it. Now my lens was somewhere in Rory's or Ronnie's stomach, and I was groping my way home.

Cutting across other people's lawns isn't something I'd normally do, but the Mendelsohns next door to us were on a month-long camping trip out west. I was tired. I wanted to get someplace quiet where I could relax and enjoy the new Agatha Potts mystery I'd started the night before, and I guess I just *spontaneously* stepped onto their grass.

That's when the tree called for help.

At first I wasn't sure it was the tree — or even if I'd heard anything at all. My steps slowed, though, and I peered around, because something had definitely registered in my brain cells. I could see well enough to tell that there wasn't anybody close by, so after a few seconds I decided that it must have been my imagination and continued on.

"Help! *Please!*"

The boughs of a giant sugar maple threw a wide band of shade over the Mendelsohns' lawn. Here and there thin rays of sun poked through and made a pattern of tiny moving dots, like disco lights on a dance floor. The voice had definitely come from somewhere up in the leaves.

"W-w-what do you want?" I stammered, feeling about as stupid as you'd expect and hoping there wouldn't be any answer.

But there was. Sort of. A rustling noise, accompanied by the sharp crack of a branch breaking and a startled gasp.

By then it was obvious that the tree wasn't talking. Someone was up there — someone with a real problem. At any moment, I half expected to see a body come plunging to the ground at my feet.

"What's the trouble?" I yelled. "Can't you get down?"

There was a long silence, and then the voice came shakily through the leaves. "That is *one* of my problems, young lady."

Young lady? It sounded like a woman. What was she doing up there in the Mendelsohns' maple? I squinted and strained. About halfway up, behind the trunk, I could just make out a shape.

"I'll get a ladder," I called. "It'll only take a minute. I live right next door. Can you hang on?"

"I fail to see that I have much choice in the matter," came the response.

"Well — uh — OK. Keep up the good work," I said, stupidly.

"Wait!" The rustling began again, this time louder. Something white flashed briefly in the upper branches.

I caught my breath. "Be careful!"

"I *am* trying," the woman said, in a frustrated sort of way. "However, it's an arduous task."

(ARDUOUS: *adjective*: difficult.)

I waited while the blurry white thing made a few attempts to find a better position, breaking off some leaves that came floating down past my nose. Finally it gave up and hung there limply, like a kite caught in the branches.

"Are you all right?" I asked anxiously.

"For the moment. But there's the question of apparel."

I knew that one. "Clothes," I said aloud.

"Exactly. Now, when you fetch the ladder, could you possibly bring a dressing gown of some kind?"

I nodded. "My mother has one. I don't know if it will fit, though. She's pretty tiny."

"That's immaterial. Any port in a storm, as they say." This attempt at humor made me feel a little better about leaving. The poor lady must have ripped whatever it was she had on. I'd done it myself, and in the same tree, too.

I raced across the rest of the Mendelsohns' yard toward my house with a lot more energy than I'd had a few minutes before. I couldn't help wishing there was somebody around to give me a hand. But it was suppertime, and all the Tucker Street families were inside the lookalike houses they called home. I'd just have to manage by myself.

I felt around in my pocket for my key, unlocked the back door, and hurried upstairs. In the bathroom, hanging from the hook on the back of the door, was my mother's blue chenille robe. I grabbed it and then went back down to the kitchen and out to the garage.

The ladder, its wooden rungs speckled with dried paint, was leaning up against the wall. Draping the robe around my neck, I slid the garage door up, then spent several minutes doing a balancing act with the ladder. All the time, though, I had the funniest feeling that somebody was playing a trick on me. It was the kind of thing the Lawler twins might have thought up, except I'd just left them with their mother. Even the Lawler twins had their limits.

I was just starting to wrestle the ladder into place against the trunk of the tree when I heard the rattle of a bicycle chain. Help at last. I turned my head and focused on the street. Blind as I was, there was no mistaking Clinton De Witt.

Clinton was a fellow eighth-grader (assuming he'd passed) at the Larson Avenue Middle School, and a real jerk. His hair was long and stringy, and he wore army clothes — big black boots with scuffed toes, baggy green pants and shirt, and a spotted fatigue cap. Every day. Maybe that was all his family could afford, but I doubted it. I think he just liked the look. He was fat and clumsy, too, and he had the annoying habit of standing where he could listen in on other people's conversations. Then he'd go around school bragging about all the secrets he knew. If I could have had anyone in the world to help me just then, Clinton would have been at the extreme bottom of my list. But any port in a storm, as I'd been reminded just minutes ago.

"Send him away!" the voice hissed before I could say anything.

Well, that solved that. My mysterious friend didn't really want Clinton around, either. By this time, though, he'd seen me with the ladder and had pulled over to the curb. Getting off his bike, he pushed his fatigue cap back on his head and came stomping across the Mendelsohns' lawn.

"Beat it, Clinton," I said — fairly diplomatically, I thought.

"I can handle this." He snatched at the ladder. I swung it out of his reach. It hit the trunk of the tree with a terrible THWACK!, sending shock waves up my arms.

"Leave me alone," I cried desperately. "You don't even know what I'm doing."

"Sure I do. Your cat's up there. That's what you have the ladder for, right?"

It made more sense than the real reason. "Uh, yeah, it's a cat, Clinton. But I can take care of it. Really."

"You're a girl," he said with a sneer. He jumped up and tried to catch one of the lower limbs. He missed by a good two feet and landed on his rear end in the grass.

Suddenly the branches started to shake violently. Clinton stared up at the tree. "Holy — What have you got, a mountain lion?"

I had to get rid of him. The poor lady up in the tree was about to have forty conniptions. If she lost her grip —

"Just about," I said hurriedly. "It's a big orange tiger cat. And he doesn't know you, Clinton. I mean, he's really vicious. He'll scratch your eyes out of your head.

There'll be blood dripping all down your face. *Your blood, Clinton.*"

He sniffed. "I've taken an emergency preparedness course."

Obviously the guy couldn't take a hint. The direct approach might be better.

"Clinton, you have no authority to be on this property. If the Mendelsohns ever saw you on their lawn in that getup, they'd think they were being invaded and call out the National Guard. You're going to end up in jail. Now *go!*"

He stared at me for a long minute. Then he said, "Crack your head open, see if I care." He spun on his heel and marched away.

"So long, Captain Commando," I muttered, and as soon as he'd pedaled off down the street and around the corner, I started up the ladder.

It bounced and jiggled under my weight. I was concentrating so hard on keeping the thing steady that I didn't look up until I reached the top rung. When I did, I nearly made one of the most *spontaneous* descents in history.

Huddled on one of the largest limbs, trying to hide as much of herself as possible behind the trunk, was an old woman. I couldn't tell *how* old, exactly, but I did know that people didn't usually get much older. But that wasn't what had startled me. Even without my contacts, I could tell that she was practically stark naked!

(NAKED: *adjective*: bare, unclothed, *unappareled!*)

11

2

The skin of the face peering around the tree trunk was softly folded, with two flushed cheeks that reminded me a little of the spiced apples they sometimes put on your dinner plate at fancy restaurants. Her pale-green eyes flickered slightly, letting me know she wasn't quite as calm as she was pretending to be. Above her eyes was a wispy fringe of snowy-white hair. It was mussed and had twigs and pieces of bark tangled in it. She was clutching the tree as if her life depended upon it. Which it did, of course.

She said nothing, but she let go with one hand long enough to reach out for the robe.

"You aren't going to try to put this on, are you?" I asked. That kind of gymnastics could be disastrous.

"I must," she said.

I took it from around my neck and passed it up to her, then turned my head away. I couldn't watch. I would have felt a little better if the fire department had been underneath with one of those nets they have for people to jump into.

She managed it somehow. The next thing I knew, she was saying, "I'm ready now," and when I glanced up again, the robe was pretty much covering the few shreds of her dark print dress that were still clinging to her body.

"Easy, now," I said. "I'll stay on the ladder right ahead of you, just in case." I didn't say in case what, but then neither of us really needed a description. I heard her take a deep breath. Then, cautiously, she eased off her perch far enough to stretch one bare foot in my direction. I grabbed it and guided it to the top rung. It was soft and smelled of soap. "Now the other one," I encouraged. "Nice and slow."

I won't go into all the details, except there were moments when I was sure we were both going to end up in a pile of broken bones. But eventually we reached the safety of the ground.

For a minute we just stood there staring at each other and trying to get our breath back. She was tall and large-boned. The sleeves of the blue robe, wrist-length on my mother, reached to just below her elbows. She clutched the two halves of the front together and fumbled with the belt.

"How did you —" I began, then decided that if it had been me standing in the middle of someone's yard practically in my birthday suit, the last thing I'd need would be to be asked for an explanation. I'd want some cover, in more ways than one. She didn't look too steady, either. In fact, I thought she was going to sit down right there on the grass. I took her arm. "You'll be a lot more comfortable at my house," I said. "Nobody's home," I added quickly.

Soon the woman was resting in a stuffed chair in our living room. I'd given her one of the small, flowered sofa cushions to tuck behind her back. I perched on the edge of the couch and watched her. The color had drained out of her cheeks. Should I call a doctor? I wondered. I'd heard of people having heart attacks out of the blue, and she sure had had reason enough.

"Are you feeling all right?" I asked, just to be on the safe side.

She shuddered, then gave a deep sigh and seemed to relax a bit. "I believe so. A few scratches, perhaps. Nothing of any consequence."

"That's good."

"That," she said fervently, "is a miracle."

She wasn't kidding. But now what? For the moment she seemed content to rest, so I left her and went into the kitchen to put on the teakettle. I figured she could use some nourishment, and I sure needed time to think. What was I going to do with her? I'd never been around old people much. All four of my grandparents had died a long time ago, even before my father. And Tucker Street wasn't exactly a retirement community. Except for Mr. Harms on the other side of us, most of the families were fairly young.

Questions kept exploding in my brain like popcorn

kernels. Questions like where did she live and how did she get up in that tree and was somebody somewhere worried about her and, most important just then, what the heck was keeping my mother? I glanced at the stove. Nearly six o'clock. Then I remembered it was Thursday. Westwinds, the small women's boutique where my mother worked, was open until eight.

Who really would have been helpful just then, of course, was Agatha Potts, the whiz-kid detective. She would have had this whole thing figured out in fifteen minutes. I'd already read three books in the series — *Amazing Agatha, Astounding Agatha,* and *Adventurous Agatha.* A couple of times I'd even managed to come up with the right solution without having to turn to the back of the book. The secret was in using your brain and looking at things a little differently than you normally did.

On second thought, why should I let all that experience go to waste when I could just as easily become Penny Eagan, Girl Sleuth? After all, here I was, smack in the middle of a mystery every bit as puzzling as the ones Agatha Potts solved. Maybe even more so. Ever since my best friend, Cherie Mathewson, had left to visit her aunt in Williamsburg, Virginia, I'd been afraid that my whole summer vacation was going to be taken up with the Lawler twins and other equally boring activities. Here was a chance to do something different. *Really* different. Then when Cherie got home and started in about Busch Gardens and all that stuff, I wouldn't have to sit there like a toad. I'd have my own excitement to share — and being a detective sure beat riding a dumb old roller coaster any day!

The teakettle whistled. I filled a cup with hot water, dropped in a flavored tea bag, and carried it back to the living room.

She was almost asleep. Her eyelids drooped, and the blue chenille robe had fallen back to reveal one bare kneecap. As soon as she heard me, though, she sat straight up and flipped the robe back into place. I pretended I hadn't noticed.

She took the cup with a grateful sigh and hands that shook a bit. Bending her head over it, she breathed in the steam. "Orange spice. How lovely." She took one sip, settled back into her chair, and murmured, "Bizarre, bizarre."

I jumped at this first clue. "You were at a bazaar?" I asked. If I knew where she'd started from, I might be able to find out how she'd ended up in a maple tree on Tucker Street.

She set the teacup down carefully on the end table beside her chair. "No, dear. But your mistake is a natural one, because you didn't hear the word in context. If I had used a proper sentence, such as 'What a bizarre day this has been,' I'm sure you would have caught the meaning."

"Strange, of course," I said.

She nodded.

My investigation wasn't going to go anyplace if she kept trying to give me grammar lessons. "But how on earth did you get in that tree?" I blurted out.

Her hands began to tremble as she reached for the teacup again. "I haven't the faintest idea." She must have realized how silly that sounded, because she continued, "I fixed myself dinner as usual and then picked up the newspaper. I remember how weary I was, reading about all those horrid little wars going on in the world. I must have dozed off. The next thing I knew, it was morning, and there I was in a tree. I have no recollection of anything in between."

"You've been there all day? But why didn't you —"

"I couldn't call out. I didn't want to attract the wrong sort of attention." The pale cheeks got pinker. "There wasn't anyone around except young children or boys, and they simply would not have done." She continued, thoughtfully, "You know, they do say one begins to reminisce about the past as one gets older, but climbing trees? That is quite ridiculous. Do you suppose I could have been sleepwalking?"

I doubted it. Old was old. But she must have managed to get up there somehow, so I figured anything was possible. "I'm sure you didn't come very far," I said — cleverly, I thought. If nothing else, I might find out where my visitor lived.

"My home is at Twenty-eight Wellington Place," she said. "It's small, but I prefer it to living in one of those mausoleums as my friend Lydia does."

(MAUSOLEUM: *noun*: a large tomb or any tomblike place.)

I knew exactly where Wellington Place was. "That's more than two miles from here!" I exclaimed. "And nobody saw you walking?"

She drew herself up. "I certainly hope not."

I looked away and chewed the skin on the side of my thumb. Her friend Lydia, she'd said. Another clue. "Could I call her for you?" I asked. "Your friend?"

"A very intelligent suggestion," the woman said briskly. "Lydia has an automobile and would be happy to pick me up. That is, if she's not engaged in a six-no-trump hand."

"Beg pardon?"

She chuckled. "A bridge term, young lady. Playing cards," she explained when I still looked blank. "Your generation isn't too familiar with it, I don't suppose, but Lydia Smith would starve herself to death rather than give up an opportunity of making slam."

"Oh." I wondered if it was anything like the thousand and one dumb slapjack games the Lawler twins were always talking me into playing. "Well, where could I call her?"

"The Beacon Manor Senior Citizen Residence. Oh, and please tell her to bring some clothing," she added as I headed for the kitchen. "Some undergarments, a pair of shoes, and maybe that black silk shift of hers, if she doesn't mind." Almost as an afterthought, she said, "I've always wanted to see how it looked on me."

"Underwear, shift, shoes," I repeated. I had the phone in my hand before I realized I didn't know who to tell Lydia Smith to pick up. In all the excitement we hadn't gotten around to introductions. "Ma'am?" Her head was nodding. I had to repeat it. "Uh, what's your name?"

She jerked awake. "Forgive me," she said, somewhat sleepily. "I'm Miss Katherine Cooper. And you are —"

"Penny. Penny Eagan."

She nodded and dropped her head again, as if it was too heavy to hold up.

Lydia Smith was home and evidently not playing tunnel or whatever, because she said she'd be delighted to take a drive on such a beautiful evening, especially with her dear friend Katherine. "But the black will not do," she trilled. "Not with her coloring. I'll bring my mauve knit. Although, confidentially," she whispered, as if Miss Cooper could hear every word, "she's put on a little weight lately. Swelling up like a watermelon, if you ask me. I do hope she doesn't stretch it out too much. Is she going out to dinner, do you know?"

"No. She had — she had an accident."

"Oh dear!"

"An accident to her . . . uh, apparel," I said quickly. Old people probably all talked the same. "She's fine, really."

"Well, I'm certainly glad of that," the woman named Lydia replied. "Oh dear, I didn't mean I was glad —"

She probably would have gone on for hours, but I said I understood and she stopped. I gave her my name and the address. First she had to find a piece of paper and a pencil to write down the directions from the mausoleum (or whatever) to Tucker Street, but finally we got it all straightened out. "It may take a little while, however," she advised me. "I'm just finishing a letter to my daughter Flory out in California, and I'd like it to go out in the morning mail." I said that would be fine, put the receiver down, and went back to the living room.

Miss Cooper was sound asleep, making little puffing noises as she exhaled. I didn't have the heart to wake her, even to tell her that Lydia Smith was coming to her rescue. She needed the rest. I took a crocheted afghan off the couch and gently covered her. She didn't move.

My stomach reminded me that I hadn't had any supper. Or lunch, either. After watching what the Lawler twins did to two perfectly good peanut butter and jelly sandwiches, I'd lost my appetite. I located a couple of leftover chicken legs, poured myself a glass of milk, and sat down at the kitchen table.

Solving real mysteries was a lot harder than trying to outguess Agatha Potts. I had a feeling this was going to take me more than fifteen minutes. So far it was like trying to do a jigsaw puzzle with half the pieces missing. The main thing, I told myself, was not to get discouraged.

It was starting to get dark by the time I finished cleaning off the last bone. I was putting the milk away when I heard the sound of a car pulling into the garage. A minute later my mother walked into the kitchen.

"I'm exhausted," she said, dropping into a chair. She slipped off her shoes and rubbed the bottoms of her feet together. "I took off a little early. What a madhouse!" She smiled up at me. "So, what did you do all day, sweetie?"

I didn't want to hit her with things too soon. "Uh, nothing," I said.

"I swear, the ladies that come into the shop are nuts," she went on, without really listening. "Mrs. Brissel tried on every dress on the rack and then informed the whole store that the things they have down the street at Fashion Parade were cheaper and just as good. I could have strangled her. Are there any more of those chicken legs in the refrigerator? I'm starved."

"Mom —"

"Never mind, honey. You probably had just as bad a day with those Lawler monsters. I'll heat up a can of soup."

"Mom, I —"

She started to unfasten the navy-blue polka-dot scarf from around her neck before she realized that I was trying to tell her something. Frowning slightly, she said, "Is something the matter, Penny?"

"Not really. Well, I mean, kinda." First things first. "I lost a lens today," I said in a rush. "Or rather, one of the Lawler twins did."

"I thought you looked a little squinty. Don't worry about it. We'll get another. You can get along with your old glasses for a few days, can't you?"

"Sure, but —"

"There's more?"

I plunged in. "Somebody's in the living room."

Her face went white. "Oh, no! Not tonight! Don't

tell me," she whispered. "It's Arthur Frank, right? That man! He refuses to accept the fact that I'm not interested in someone who's been married three times. Can't you get rid of him? I suppose not. He must know I'm here."

"It's not Mr. Frank, Mom. It's — it's an old lady."

"Really?"

"Shhh!" I hissed. "She's right in there sleeping. You'll wake her up."

"Sleeping? Come on, Penny, isn't it a little late for April Fools' jokes?"

"It's not a joke." Quickly I filled her in on how I'd found Miss Cooper. As she listened, she began to giggle. By the time I got to the part where Lydia Smith was talking about her friend's swelling up like a watermelon, it was all she could do to control herself.

"This I've just got to see!" she cried, heading for the door. I stayed where I was. She was gone for a few minutes, then she walked slowly back into the kitchen.

"Is Miss Cooper still asleep?" I asked.

My mother gave me an odd look. "She may be. Wherever she is. Whoever she is."

"What do you mean?"

"Penny, there's no one in there."

I raced to the living room. The stuffed chair was empty, and lying on the floor in a crumpled heap, on top of the afghan, was the blue chenille robe.

3

My mother was convinced I'd made it up. I could do something more constructive with my time, she said. I was probably just looking for some extra attention because I didn't have a father like most other kids. (She'd been known to go on a guilt trip about that every once in a while, although so far she'd never felt bad enough to do anything about it.)

I couldn't really blame her for not believing me. It was an awful lot to ask someone to accept — a practically naked old lady who'd been stuck in a tree and who'd then disappeared (still practically naked) from a chair in your living room. I was having trouble with it myself. I searched the house from attic to basement, but there was no sign of Miss Katherine Cooper.

I was all ready to continue looking outside when my mother stopped me.

"But I have to find her, Mom! She's old and she hardly has any clothes on."

"Penny, that's enough. I realize I've probably been

leaving you on your own too much, but you have to understand it's been difficult for me, too."

In the end, two things saved me. First, my mother was well aware that I didn't have the greatest imagination in the world. My writing assignments, a few teachers had kindly pointed out, were about as interesting as the used-car ads in the newspaper.

Second, the doorbell rang.

On the steps was Lydia Smith (*Mrs.* Lydia Smith, she informed us), complete with a tan overnight case that held, I supposed, the mauve knit dress and the other things Miss Cooper had requested.

Lydia Smith didn't look quite as old as her missing friend, but when I tried to explain that Miss Cooper had pulled a vanishing act, she put on a couple of years real fast.

"But where did she go?" she asked several times, until my mother steered her toward the kitchen and sat her down at the table.

Lydia Smith must have been gorgeous when she was young. She was still beautiful, though in a different way. She was nearly as tall as Miss Cooper and wore her hair in soft curls all over her head. It was quite black, with a few streaks of white running through it, so that it looked frosted. She was wearing a very attractive dusty-rose dress of some shiny material, and over her shoulders was draped a lacy white shawl. I could see my mother eyeing her admiringly, even though she was pretty confused about what was going on.

I told Mrs. Smith as much as I dared, leaving out

those parts that I thought would upset her. Which was practically everything. "I was coming home from baby-sitting," I said, "and I met Miss Cooper . . . uh, in front of the Mendelsohns' house. She said she was lost. So I asked her if she wanted to come inside."

"Katherine knows this city like the back of her hand," Mrs. Smith declared when I'd finished. "I'm sure she got her bearings and just went home. If you don't mind, I'll give her a call."

She fished around in her purse and came up with a small address book. "Katherine's number is unlisted," she explained. "It's much safer for people living alone."

But there was no answer at the house on Wellington Place, and now Lydia Smith began to get worried. Finally my mother offered to search the neighborhood by car. Twenty minutes later she was back. No luck. For all any of us knew, Miss Cooper had totally vanished off the face of the earth.

Mrs. Smith thought we should alert the police. "The poor thing must have been terribly confused to wander off like that," she said, adding confidentially, "It does happen, you know. Dear me, if she had to give up her place, I think it would just about kill her."

I could see that my mother was in no mood to go messing around with the police, but it was the only sensible move.

"The police have more important things on their minds," my mother said after hanging up the phone. "The desk sergeant said there've been four break-ins and an armed robbery in the last two hours, and the chief's father-in-law just took one of the patrol cars for a joyride. I gave the sergeant our number. He said he'd issue a lookout bulletin, and if Miss Cooper still isn't back by morning, someone can go in and file an official missing-person report. I'm afraid there's not much more we can do." She sneezed.

"Oh dear. Do you have a cold?" Mrs. Smith asked, alarmed.

"I don't think so," my mother said, and immediately sneezed again.

Mrs. Smith edged her chair away from the table and fiddled with the fringe on her shawl. I wondered why she seemed so worried about a couple of little cold germs. "You're right, of course," she said then. "But I hate to think of Katherine being out there all alone." Her eyes filled.

"I'm sure she'll call you later," my mother said, "and if she doesn't . . ." She left it hanging.

Lydia Smith thanked us for the tea, picked up the overnight case, and hurried out to her car.

My mother made me go through the whole story again, including the part about the tree, while she drank some chicken bouillon. "That has to be the most outlandish thing I've ever heard," she declared when I'd finished. "Of course, some older people go around the bend and do odd things. Still, if what you told me is true, I don't get the impression that she's too unbalanced."

I picked up her empty cup and carried it to the dishwasher. "That's just it, Mom," I said. "She was upset, sure — who wouldn't be? But she seemed to be thinking straight. She used a bunch of big words I didn't even understand."

"Like *bedtime*?" my mother asked with a grin that turned into a yawn. "Honey, I'm beat. We can't do any more tonight. I have to be at the shop early." She let out another sneeze. "Oh, Lord! The last thing I need is a cold. I'm turning in."

I tossed around all night. Toward morning I found myself dreaming that I was chasing twin maple trees around a forest with a chain saw. I woke up to the sound of my mother's hair dryer in the next room. When it shut off, I just lay there, listening to the soft breeze as it ruffled the curtains on my window.

My mother stuck her head into my room just before she left for work. She said she'd call Eyes Right Opticians and order me a new lens. She also mentioned that it had rained during the night but said the sun was out now, and if I didn't have anything else to do, it might be a good time to weed the garden. I couldn't get too excited about grubbing around in the mud, and then I thought about the Lawler twins and realized that things could have been an awful lot worse. At least dirt stayed where you put it.

A light bulb went off in my head. Dirt! Maybe Miss Cooper had left footprints in the garden and I could follow her tracks.

I dug my old glasses out of my desk drawer. There was a safety pin holding the hinge together on one earpiece. It felt funny to be wearing frames again. I scrambled into my jeans, the ones with the frayed cuffs that came up to my ankles, tossed down a half-empty glass of orange juice that my mother had left on the kitchen counter, and headed out the back door and around to the edge of the garden under the living-room windows.

There wasn't any trace of footprints. I suppose I hadn't really expected that there would be, but it would have been nice. In that respect Agatha Potts had a head start on me. I didn't have a writer to sprinkle clues around for me to trip over.

I plucked at a couple of weeds, which were bigger than the flowers. The rain had softened the ground, and they came out easily. I kept going and soon had a good-sized pile. But all the time I kept thinking about how weird last night had been and wondering if Miss Cooper had made it home.

When I was finished, I raked all the weeds together, along with a zinnia plant or two that I'd yanked up by mistake, and got a plastic lawn bag from the garage. As I bent over to stuff everything in, an electric whine started up in the next yard. I looked up to see Mr. Harms come gliding down his back-door ramp in his motorized wheelchair, the sun reflecting off his nearly bald head. Behind him hobbled Barney, his old, stiff-legged dog. They were a funny pair, and I hid a smile as Barney wandered over to poke his graying snout through the fence.

"How's the arthritis today, Mr. Harms?" I called out, giving Barney's nose a pat.

The wheelchair ground to a halt on the drive.

"Dampness doesn't help it much," he grumbled. "'Course Barney here, he's got the same complaint. In dog years, he's way older than me, you know." He let out a cackle.

I laughed, too. Mr. Harms didn't let his handicap get him down. He'd refused to give up his pet store, even after his legs had gotten so bad. His sons wanted him to come live with them, but he said he'd been born independent and was going to stay independent as long as he could. He could still get around well enough to take care of himself in the house. The wheelchair gave him the freedom go to other places, too. And people on Tucker Street were good about checking in on him every now and then to see if he needed anything.

Every afternoon, unless the weather was really lousy, Mr. Harms scooted down Tucker Street and over the four blocks to his shop, the Green Lizard, on Tenth Avenue. (The store was named for a big, scaly iguana called Tico-Tico, who lived in the front window.) He had somebody to help him with the heavy work, but mostly he ran the place himself.

I changed the subject. "Going to the store today?"

"Gonna have to," he replied. "My boy that cleans the cages up and quit on me last week. But I think I'll grab myself a nap first. I'm a bit tired after being up two nights running with a howling mutt."

"Is something the matter with Barney?" I asked in dismay. The dog looked lively enough. Just then he was interested in an orange and black Monarch butterfly that was flitting around the fence.

"Oh, he just gets excited if he smells some other animal around. People ought to learn to keep their pets in the house at night."

I wondered whose animal had been out. Probably that black poodle down the street who constantly left little presents on our lawn.

Mr. Harms switched on his chair again and drove over to the side of his house to inspect his roses.

I finished putting the weeds in the bag, put a twist-tie on it, and set it down next to the garbage cans. Then I went in to wash up. I was just scraping the last bits of dirt from under my fingernails and thinking maybe I should try to call Lydia Smith at Beacon Manor when my mother phoned from the shop.

"I forgot to tell you," she said. "Some of the girls are going out bowling after work. I know I promised last night not to leave you alone so much, but I already said I'd go with them. Do you mind?"

Of course I didn't, I told myself. It had been eight years since my father died. My mother was only thirty-six, too young to be stuck in the house with just me for the rest of her life. But I wanted her to have fun, not waste her time bowling with "the girls." Occasionally she had real dates, like the insurance salesman who'd dumped her the day after she signed up for a policy. Then there was the guy who'd promised to get her a job in the movies. The job had turned out to be a two-second commercial in which she zipped up an escalator with about fifty other people. She went by so fast that all you could see was a blur. And let's not forget Arthur Frank, the three-time loser. So I couldn't blame her for being a bit suspicious of men. But sometimes I couldn't help thinking about how nice it would be to have one around, just to make things interesting. And sometimes I even wondered what it would be like to have a stepfather. But I didn't want to make my mother feel any guiltier than she already did, so I never brought up the subject.

I went back outside and sat on the porch, stretching my legs down the steps and leaning back to let the sun shine on my face. I closed my eyes. A bunch of spots swam around on the back of my eyelids. They reminded me of the disco lights on the Mendelsohns' lawn, and then of course that got me going about Miss Cooper again.

"Get your cat down?"

Clinton De Witt was standing on the walk, his stupid fatigue cap pulled down so far over his ears that his straight brown hair stuck out around the bottom like fringe on a blanket.

I sighed. Why was he hanging around all of a sudden? "No problem, Clinton. Came right to me."

"My aunt had a cat like that. They finally had to put her bed up in the tree."

"Your aunt's?"

"No. The cat's. They made a little platform, kind of like a tree fort, you know? The cat stayed up there all the time, except when it was time to eat."

"Interesting," I muttered. I didn't believe him for a minute, but then, what would he have thought about my naked-lady story?

I figured that now that the Great Cat Question had

been answered, he'd go away. He didn't. Without even being invited, he sat right down next to me on the step. If he thought he was going to pick up any juicy bits of gossip from me, he was in for a long wait. After what seemed like three years of silence, he said, "You look funny."

Nice kid. "I'm wearing glasses. I lost one of my contacts."

"Oh."

We sat there some more. Finally I said, "Don't you have something else to do?" I didn't mean it exactly the way it sounded. I was just curious about what Rambo did in his spare time.

"Like what?"

"I don't know. Do you play baseball?"

"That's for wimps."

"Soccer?"

No answer.

"Well, do you swim?"

"Do you?"

"Swim? Sure."

"So do I."

Yeah, the dead man's float, I thought to myself, looking at the stomach that bulged over his belt buckle. Some army. If there was going to be a war, we'd be much better off having it before Clinton got old enough to be a real soldier.

I didn't say anything else for a long time. A *very* long time. I wanted him to get bored enough to leave. But he stayed.

Just then the kid who delivers the weekly advertising circulars came up the street, a newspaper bag slung over his shoulder. He grinned as he saw Clinton and me on the step.

"Think fast!" he yelled, and he whipped a rolled-up paper toward us. It sailed straight for Clinton's head. I waited for him to make a move to catch it. When it became evident that he wasn't about to, I lunged and made a one-handed grab.

I stared at Clinton. He was crouched into a ball, with his knees drawn up as close as they could get to his chest and his arms crossed in front of his face.

"It's all right. I saved you," I said sarcastically.

He peeked out, then slowly lowered his arms. His face was as red as a suit of long johns. "I'm going home," he announced stiffly. He stood up and slouched off down the walk, toward where his bike lay against the curb. As he neared the street, his back straightened and the heels of his boots clicked in a rhythm that almost made me want to grab a flag and fall in behind him.

"Hey Clinton!" I called.

He kept marching.

It was obvious that Clinton wasn't anything like the big GI Joe he pretended to be. Sure, on the surface he appeared all macho, but underneath he was about as tough as a handful of cottage cheese. Now he was mad because I'd seen what a coward he really was.

I couldn't help feeling a little sorry for him. "Clinton!" I yelled again, but he'd already picked up his bike and was getting ready to swing his leg over the seat. Well, I wasn't going to get down on my knees in the middle of Tucker Street and plead with him. If he wanted to be snotty, that was his problem. "Aw, go get a job," I muttered.

The words were hardly out of my mouth when it struck me. Somewhere, Clinton had lost his self-confidence. Well, a detective is supposed to be good at finding things that are lost, right? Even if I hadn't had much success at finding Miss Cooper yet, that didn't mean I couldn't work on another case at the same time. And this one was practically going to solve itself.

"Wait!" I slid off the steps, dashed down the walk, and grabbed his handlebars. "Clinton, how would you like a job?"

He stared at me as if he'd never heard the word before. Quickly, I filled him in about Mr. Harms and about how the boy who cleaned the pet cages had just quit. "I bet he'd hire you in a minute. He could really use the help, Clinton."

I wondered if anybody had ever really needed Clinton before, because the idea took so long to sink in.

"It won't hurt to talk to him, will it?" I pressed, pulling his sleeve. "He's home right now."

He didn't move.

"Come *on*." I tugged harder.

He yanked himself free. "Stop bugging me, will you?" But finally he got off his bike and started across the lawn toward Mr. Harms' driveway, making sure, though, that he had the last word. "I'm only doing this because I need some cash."

4

Mr. Harms was snipping dead blossoms from his rosebushes. In the middle of the driveway, Barney dozed on the sun-warmed concrete. When I introduced Clinton and explained my idea about his taking over the job at the pet store, Mr. Harms grunted and began sizing Clinton up. He started at the toes of his army boots and ended with his fatigue cap.

"Kind of young to be in the military, aren't you?" he said finally.

"Uh —"

"Clinton's not really a soldier," I broke in. "He's in middle school. Like me."

"Well, it don't matter. Can you handle a broom?"

Clinton's face went blank.

"Sure he can, Mr. Harms," I said. "You've heard of brooms, haven't you, Clinton? They have handles and a bunch of straw —"

"The boy doesn't need your tongue, Penny Eagan,"

Mr. Harms growled. "He's got one of his own. Least-wise, I guess he does. What about it, son?"

"Uh, no, sir. I mean, yes, sir. I mean, of course I know what a broom is. But Penny said I'd be working with animals."

Mr. Harms cackled. "Wherever you have animals, boy, brooms go right along with 'em."

Clinton got the picture. His nose wrinkled.

"It won't be that bad," I told him. "He can do it, Mr. Harms. Just look at the great muscles he has." Fat was more like it, but I hoped Mr. Harms wouldn't notice. "And I know you'll find Clinton extremely reliable."

You could almost hear the bones lock into place as Clinton snapped to attention.

"Hmmm. Guess we could give it a try," Mr. Harms said at last. "I pay twenty-five dollars. That's for two afternoons a week and all day Saturday. Think you can handle it?"

"Yes, sir!"

He told Clinton to be at the Green Lizard at one o'clock that afternoon. "I open at three. You'll need time to clean up and learn where things are."

I walked Clinton out to the street. "See how easy that was? Boy, I sure wish I had a better job for the summer. Baby-sitting is the pits."

Clinton eyed me suspiciously. "Then how come you didn't take the one at the pet store yourself?"

"Because my mom's allergic to just about every animal on the face of the earth. Except penguins, maybe." It was the truth, but more than that, I didn't want him to think I was trying to talk him into something. Even though I was.

He seemed satisfied with that. "It's lunchtime," he said abruptly.

"OK," I said. "Good luck this afternoon."

He muttered something as he got on his bike and rode off.

I went back into the house and up to my room. I started throwing out notes and other stuff from school that was still cluttering up my desk. When I was done, I had a whole drawer that I could use for my detective work. All I needed was some files. A couple of old notebooks with the used pages ripped out did the trick. I printed Clinton's name on the cover of one. Inside I jotted down the date he'd been hired by Mr. Harms, what hours he was supposed to work, and what the pay was.

I settled back in my chair and chewed on the eraser of my pencil. For the first time all summer I felt like I'd accomplished something. Because of me, Mr. Harms now had some help in the Green Lizard and Clinton would be too busy to think about his image. It hadn't been too hard, either. As Agatha Potts said at least once every twenty pages or so, "It's not where you look, it's what you see."

I turned back to the notebook. There didn't seem to be anything more to say about Clinton, so I nearly wrote "Case Closed" at the end. But I didn't. And a good thing, too, as it turned out.

Miss Cooper's case was proving to be more of a challenge. In her "file," I entered the following:

Subject: Katherine Cooper. Rescued same from Mendelsohns' maple on Thursday, July 16. Disappeared from Eagan residence later that day.
Present whereabouts: unknown.
Contact: Mrs. Lydia Smith.
Address: Beacon Manor Senior Citizen Residence.

I'd just remembered that I wanted to call Lydia Smith to see if she'd heard anything when the phone rang downstairs. I raced to answer it.

"This is Miss Cooper," a prim voice said in my ear.

"Miss Cooper!" I cried. "Where are you?"

"At Beacon Manor, of course," she replied, as if to say, where else?

"Then you're all right?"

"Yes, thank you, young lady. Lydia insisted I call. I'm afraid everyone has been left with the impression that I've suddenly become senile. I want to assure you that I'm perfectly all right."

(SENILE: *adjective*: exhibiting a loss of mental faculties, associated with old age.)

"But —"

"I'll be happy to tell you about it," she interrupted. "I promised my friends I'd play a round of bridge just now, but I'd like to thank you in person for coming to my rescue yesterday. Do you think you could join Lydia and me for lunch in about an hour?"

Could I! This was just what I needed — a chance to get all the puzzle pieces together in one place.

Miss Cooper was pleased I wanted to come. She gave me directions to Beacon Manor, which was on

Stafford Avenue. It wasn't exactly around the corner, but it was near enough for me to get there by bike. I changed into a pair of tan cotton slacks and a yellow camp shirt, clipped the sides of my hair back with barrettes, and tied my jacket around my waist. Then I took my copy of *Amazing Agatha* out of the bookcase and compared myself to the picture on the cover. Agatha Potts was tall, with short, light hair and blue eyes, and she was wearing a baggy cotton sweater over blue shorts. She also had a magnifying glass. The only thing we had in common was glasses, though hers didn't have a safety pin holding them together.

The Beacon Manor Senior Citizen Residence didn't look like a tomb at all. It was more like a plantation. The middle part, which was two stories of light-colored brick, had a wide front porch with white pillars. Two wings stuck out from either side of it. An enormous lawn, neatly mown and dotted with lovely old trees, sloped gently down to the street.

I rode up the circular drive and parked my bike by some bushes near the porch, making sure it was off the walk so no one would trip over it. As I climbed the front steps, I could see six or seven older people sitting in big wooden chairs, talking or just gazing out at the scenery. Some of them nodded to me. I nodded back, feeling a little like a grape in a box of raisins.

Just inside the door, an attractive woman about my mother's age was seated behind a desk. I looked at the name plate. JESSICA BITTERMAN: MANAGER. She raised her eyes from her paperwork and gave me a pleasant smile. "You must be Penny," she said. "Katherine said she was expecting a young visitor. She and Lydia are in the dining room. Just go straight down this hall. It's the third door on the right."

I thanked her and started off in the direction she'd indicated. A tan carpet muffled my footsteps. Now I was beginning to understand why Miss Cooper felt the way she did about the place. I could almost hear the clocks ticking on the wall. And it was as super-clean as a hospital. I would've felt more comfortable if there had been a few magazines lying around on the tables, or even a crumpled gum wrapper. Or a speck of dust. I wondered what the people who lived here did for excitement. Probably sat around and watched the sun fade the curtains.

Suddenly a delicious smell crept into my nose. As I followed it, I heard a low buzzing, sort of what you'd get if you stood next to a cherry tree in full bloom. I stopped at a door marked Dining Room and peered around the corner.

The room held about twenty small tables. Most of them were filled with elderly people. They were eating from plastic containers with plastic forks and knives and drinking from plastic cups, so there wasn't any sound of dishes clattering, only the rather pleasant hum of voices. I couldn't see Miss Cooper. I edged inside the room, hoping she'd spot me and wave or something. Instead, a little old lady with thin white hair and wire-rimmed glasses perched on her nose came lurching toward me on unsteady legs.

"Are you lost, dear?" she asked, rather hopefully.

"Let me show you where the front desk is." She grabbed my arm with a surprisingly strong grip and started half pulling, half pushing me back down the hallway. I told her I'd already been there, but she paid no attention. There didn't seem to be any polite way of prying myself loose.

A tall man with a salt-and-pepper brush cut, wearing a red plaid shirt, came strolling toward us.

"Good afternoon, Alice," he said jauntily. "Would this be your granddaughter?" He gave me an elegant bow.

Alice jerked me to a halt. "The child is lost," she said briskly. "I'm taking her to Miss Bitterman." She rocked back on her heels and prepared to take off again.

"Actually, I'm looking for Miss Katherine Cooper," I managed to get out.

"Ah." A look of understanding came over the man's face. "I believe I saw Kitty in the dining room a short while ago. The young lady can find her own way," he told Alice, "but if you're going to your room, I'll walk with you, if I may." With that, he eased Alice's hand from my arm and tucked it firmly into his own elbow. Then he winked at me and started off down the hall at a slow pace, with Alice clinging to him like a burr.

I headed back toward the dining room. At the door I nearly bumped into Miss Cooper.

"There you are!" she cried. "I thought I saw you a minute ago, and then you disappeared."

Now we're even, I thought to myself, but out loud I said, "Some lady thought I was lost."

"Alice Pringle, no doubt," she said. "Well, you're here. Come in and sit down. We have your lunch all ready."

She threaded her way slowly through the room to a table in the back, where Lydia Smith was impatiently fingering the top of a plastic foam container. Two similar boxes, along with plastic tableware and cups and paper napkins, marked places for Miss Cooper and me. One of the cups had coffee in it; the other was full of what appeared to be lemonade. I figured the lemonade was for me.

"Alice Pringle abducted her," Miss Cooper explained as she lowered herself into her own chair. "The poor thing is getting worse."

Mrs. Smith sniffed. "You're much too easy on her, Katherine. I don't know how much longer we can close our eyes to that nuisance. I should think Miss Bitterman would say something to the board of directors." Seeing my puzzled expression, she whispered, "Alice is a hitchhiker."

"A hitchhiker?" I echoed.

"She doesn't walk very well," Miss Cooper said. "There's a rule here that if you can't take care of yourself, you must go elsewhere. Usually a nursing home. Everyone fights that. It's like the last step to the grave. Alice pretends she's fine, and so far she's managed to keep up the illusion by inventing excuses to latch onto other people. That's how she gets places."

"Just last week," Mrs. Smith put in, "she had the nerve to suggest that I needed help going to the laundry room. Why, I can still climb a flight of stairs as well as when I was forty!"

I thought of Mr. Harms in his own house and felt sorry for Alice Pringle.

Miss Cooper cut in briskly. "That's enough gloom and doom, Lydia. I think we'd better proceed with our meal while it's still hot."

The plastic containers each held a broiled pork chop, an ice cream scoop of mashed potatoes with warm, brown gravy over the top, a helping of limp green beans, a paper cup full of apple sauce, and a small chunk of chocolate cake.

While I ate, I stole a good look at Miss Cooper, who, for a change, was dressed. She had on royal-blue slacks and a matching knit top. Her short hair was neatly combed, and she wore a touch of makeup. She didn't seem like the same person I'd found in the Mendelsohns' maple the day before. There were a thousand things I wanted to ask her, but I thought I'd better wait until she was ready to talk about it.

She must have sensed my curiosity, though, because as soon as she was finished eating, she put down her fork and said to me, "I'm so glad you could come. Lydia and I have been wearing our brains out over this thing until we can't think anymore. Isn't that right, Lydia?"

Lydia Smith bobbed her head up and down as if she was afraid she might miss something on her plate if

she talked. Finally she gave up trying to do two things at once and stopped eating. "Of course, I didn't know the whole story until Katherine told me," she said, looking at me in an insulted sort of way.

I concentrated on my forkful of cake.

"Now, despite the fact that Katherine says she's fine, I don't think we can afford to ignore what has happened." After picking the last tiny bit of meat off her chop, Mrs. Smith crumpled her napkin, piled everything except her coffee cup into the now-empty container, and snapped the lid shut. "Katherine, would you mind very much taking these to the trash bin? I hate messy tables."

Miss Cooper opened her mouth to say something, then thought better of it. "Certainly, Lydia. You've been such a help to me. I don't know what I'd do without you."

"Here, let me get it," I said, starting up.

"No, dear. You're our guest," Mrs. Smith said firmly. "Katherine can manage quite well."

I thought it was strange that she wouldn't accept my offer even though obviously I could get around much faster than either of them. But when Miss Cooper had gathered up all the trash and was walking across the room toward a large barrel, I understood. Mrs. Smith leaned over and whispered, "I'm quite concerned about Katherine. You see, she doesn't have any relatives, and she insists on living alone in that big, old house, eighty-two or no eighty-two. When she called this morning, straightaway I told her to come over here and stay with me for a while. They allow us to have overnight guests, and she already belongs to the Senior Citizens' Club that meets here. You see, she hardly remembers anything about yesterday — except for your house and being in that tree."

My chances of solving the mystery seemed to be dwindling. If Miss Cooper couldn't give me any more clues as to what had really happened, I was sunk. "It's bizarre," I said. My detective skills weren't going to dazzle anyone, that was for sure. Maybe my vocabulary would.

Mrs. Smith nodded wisely. "Mildred Toomey went like that. One minute she was as sane as I am, and the next . . . Katherine seems all right now, but —" She broke off suddenly and then continued in a different tone, "— so my daughter Flory went out to live in California, and — Oh, there you are, Katherine! Thank you so much!"

Miss Cooper sat back down and rested her arms on the table. I sipped my lemonade and waited to hear her story.

"I woke up this morning in my own bed," she began. "I'll tell you, it was quite a relief. I thought perhaps the whole incident had been a horrid dream, but when I called Lydia to tell her about it, she informed me that it was quite real. And then later I found what remained of my good dress." The memory of it made her shudder.

"Katherine was very upset," Mrs. Smith said, unnecessarily.

"I still am! To fall asleep — not once, but twice! And then to wake up and not recall where I'd been, well . . . I hate to admit it, but I'm almost afraid of being by myself."

"Then you must put your name on the list for Beacon Manor." Mrs. Smith set down her coffee. "It's all very well to be independent, as I've told you many times, Katherine. However, there's nothing wrong with letting someone else look out for your welfare, especially when you're getting on in years."

After her put-down of Beacon Manor the day before, I expected to hear an argument from Miss Cooper, but she hesitated.

"There has to be some logical explanation for all of this," I broke in. "Maybe you should see a doctor."

"Or a nutritionist," put in Mrs. Smith, quickly latching onto the idea. "They've become very popular. And they do say you are what you eat. Now, Charles, my husband, was terribly overweight." She sighed. "I told him he was chewing his way to an early funeral, and he finally discovered how right I was. Although it was much too late, of course."

My stomach rumbled. I scraped my chair on the floor to cover up the sound.

"It might not hurt to try," Mrs. Smith continued. "Why, I understand that eating the right food can even improve your memory. Just think of all the things you could remember, Katherine! You know you're always complaining about that."

Miss Cooper shuddered. "There are some things, Lydia dear, that should remain *perdu*."

(I've looked through three dictionaries and still can't find that one. I don't think it's English.)

"Not to change the subject," she went on, changing the subject, "but we've been going on about me and woefully neglecting our visitor."

I wondered if maybe she was ignoring my idea about a doctor because she was afraid of what she might find out. I didn't want to keep pushing the issue, though, so I started telling them about myself and about how my father had died when I was six. They both clucked their tongues a lot and said what a shame it was.

"I was quite a bit older when Charles passed on," Lydia Smith said, "but it was a shock just the same. For the longest time I didn't know what to do with myself."

"You should have had a career to fall back on," Miss Cooper said bruskly. She was back to her old self again. "I have always been a great believer in education for women."

"Oh, it's not all that much of an advantage, Katherine," retorted her friend. "Look at you. You educated yourself right out of a husband." She turned to me. "Men don't want their wives to be smarter than they are."

Miss Cooper drew herself up even straighter, if that was possible. "It was quite the other way around, Lydia dear. I had more sense than to spend my life picking up after some helpless male. I preferred to pursue a more enlightened profession."

It was like watching a Ping-Pong match. On the

surface it all seemed friendly enough, but I could almost feel the zaps as they landed. "A lot of women get married and have a job, too, now," I said.

They both nodded their heads, as if to say, "How lovely," except I could tell neither one of them meant it.

"Where did you work?" I asked Miss Cooper.

"I was an instructor at the Welton Normal School for Teachers. I taught grammar and elocution."

"Elocu—" My tongue got tangled up.

"El-o-*cu*-tion," she pronounced. "Simply speaking, that is the art of effective communication. It's gone out of favor somewhat, I'm afraid. People don't care what they say these days."

"The world is going to hell in a handbasket," murmured Mrs. Smith

"*Lydia!*"

"I'm only repeating what Charles used to tell me, Katherine. Although I grant you his speech *was* a bit earthy." And a faraway smile touched her lips.

5

Miss Cooper and Lydia walked me to the front door and came out onto the porch. A few of the residents were strolling along the driveway under the shade of the trees, but most of the chairs were empty.

"Nap time," Mrs. Smith remarked to no one in particular.

Leaning against the porch railing was the man in the red plaid shirt, the one who had rescued me from the clutches of Alice the Hitchhiker. As I started to say my goodbyes, he caught my eye.

"I see you found your quarry," he said.

Miss Cooper said, "I didn't realize you two had met, Edward."

"Indeed we have. In the hall. Alice was catching a ride. I managed to intercept them before they ended up lost forever in the wilds of the boiler room." He chuckled. "However, we weren't formally introduced. Edward Netterich." He held out his hand.

"Penny Eagan," I said, taking it. It was warm and firm.

"Edward is my bridge partner," Miss Cooper explained.

"Except for this morning. I had some errands to run and missed the game. How did it go?"

"Not terribly exciting," Miss Cooper said. "Marion Haberley took your place. Anna and Lydia did make game twice in succession — which, of course, made Anna absolutely euphoric."

(EUPHORIC: *adjective*: extremely happy.)

"It's not that we played particularly well," added Lydia. "We just had the cards."

"Bathtub running the wrong way?" Mr. Netterich said to Miss Cooper.

I stared blankly at them.

"It's an old wives' tale," he explained. "They say partners who are facing the same direction the bathtub is facing get better cards."

"Oh." It still didn't make any sense.

"We had a good round Wednesday, though, didn't we, Kitty? I've never seen Anna as furious as she was when you were sitting there with that ace and she thought she had a grand slam."

Mrs. Smith giggled — a rather strange sound coming from an older person, I thought. "She almost strangled on those beads of hers. Honestly, Katherine, I don't know why you surprised her like that. You could have doubled and made ever so many more points."

"I was getting rather tired of her uppity attitude," Miss Cooper said firmly. "One would think she was the World Bridge Champion."

"For a minute I thought she was going to get physical," Mrs. Smith said — almost wistfully, it seemed to me.

Edward Netterich sucked in his cheeks and made a birdlike face. "You vill regret zis someday, you she-cat," he hissed. "Zat I can promise you!" And he burst out laughing. I did, too. Even Miss Cooper allowed herself a smile.

Miss Cooper explained, "Anna Krevotsky is one of the residents here. She takes her bridge very seriously."

"Not that we don't," Edward Netterich added hastily, "but losing a hand here and there isn't going to bring about the downfall of civilization."

Lydia Smith frowned. "I enjoy being her partner, Edward. Oh, I admit she is a little overdramatic at times, but that's how people are in that funny little European country she's from. Dear me, I never can remember the name of it."

"Transylvania," leered Mr. Netterich. "Where the vampires live."

"That's not very nice, Edward."

"I was just joking, Lydia. But those costumes she wears *are* just a bit ostentatious."

(OSTENTATIOUS: *adjective*: gaudy, theatrical.)

"And completely unsuitable for her age," added Miss Cooper primly.

They were having fun. In a way they reminded me of the kids at school. It surprised me. I'd thought that when you got old you stopped being silly, but apparently not.

"Well, I'd better get going," I said. They all smiled and told me to come back and visit soon. I said I would. Aside from the fact that I still hadn't found out why Miss Cooper had been in the Mendelsohns' tree, I was really worried about her. I couldn't give up on her now.

"And thank you once again for your assistance," Miss Cooper said. "You're a lovely young lady, and a true friend in need."

"Trouble, Kitty?" asked Mr. Netterich, who had overheard this last comment.

Lydia Smith jumped in. "Katherine had a little spell, Edward. I told her she ought to have Miss Bitterman put her name on the list right away, because you know how long it takes to get an apartment, but she —"

"That will do, Lydia," Miss Cooper interrupted. "I'm not going to make any hasty decisions. I feel perfectly fine."

"The hazards of growing old," Mr. Netterich muttered, but he didn't ask any more questions.

I went down the steps, unlocked my bike, and pedaled off down the driveway, leaving the three of them standing on the porch.

I was riding down Tenth Avenue, hugging the curb to avoid getting run over, when I passed the Green Lizard Pet Store. Its door was standing wide open.

Clinton's bike was chained to a light post outside. I had an urge to stop and check on how he was getting along with Mr. Harms, but I resisted it. Since there didn't seem to be a stampede of animals pouring onto the sidewalk, I figured he couldn't be doing too badly. Better leave well enough alone.

My room was just as I'd left it, with my files still on the desk. I jotted down a few things in Clinton's folder about his showing up for work the first day and how everything seemed normal.

I gnawed on my thumbnail. What was I going to do about Miss Cooper's problem? A whole day had gone by, and I still wasn't any closer to an answer. There had to be one. I was sure of it. People didn't go climbing trees for no reason. Well, kids did, but usually not grown-ups. And certainly not grown-grown-ups like Miss Cooper. But what other reason could there be, except that she might be getting — what was that word? — *senile*? Forgetful. And I didn't want to think about that.

Suddenly I realized where I'd been going wrong. I'd been searching for an obvious answer. The secret, I reminded myself, was not in where you looked, but in what you saw. Something could be sticking out as plain as the nose on my face, and I was missing it completely. I picked up my pencil and opened Miss Cooper's file.

OK, think about it for a minute, I told myself. Crazy or not, why would a person go up in a tree?

1. *To pick fruit.*

In an apple tree, maybe. Not the Mendelsohns' maple.

2. *To escape a wild animal.*

Unlikely. A bear did get loose from the zoo a few years back, but within five minutes, they had a pack of bloodhounds, the ASPCA, both candidates for mayor, and an assortment of reporters and photographers hot on its trail.

3. *To eavesdrop on someone.*

They do it on TV all the time. But again, unlikely. The Mendelsohns' maple is fifty feet away from their house, which was empty at the time anyway, and since when was the CIA hiring eighty-two-year-old spies?

4. *To be in a movie about the Incredible Hulk.*

Miss Cooper was playing the part of his mother. Her clothes *were* in shreds, and — Dumb, dumber, dumbest.

5. *Because of drugs.*

Now I might be getting somewhere. I didn't mean that Miss Cooper just couldn't say no, but older people were often on medication for something or other. What if Miss Cooper's strange behavior was just a bad side effect?

A breeze blew in my open window. I was hot and tired after my long bike ride, and all that thinking was making me dizzy. I put my head down on my desk and shut my eyes, just for a minute. The next thing I knew, there was a loud pounding going on.

"*Mffff?*" I asked out of a deep fog.

The sun was slanting in my window. It had to be pretty late in the day. The pounding continued, but now I realized it was someone at the front door. I pried my eyes open and groped my way downstairs. A boy was outside on the front step.

"We don't need any," I mumbled.

He hesitated. "Need any what?"

"Magazi—" I began, then stopped and peered closer. "Clinton?"

He grinned — euphorically.

It wasn't hard to see why I'd mistaken him for some kid working his way through school. The green army pants and shirt were clean and pressed and looked almost like regular clothes. He'd misplaced the fatigue cap and combed his hair back out of his eyes. You could tell he'd even made an effort to trim the back, because although it was still pretty scraggly, it was an inch or so shorter. And his big clodhoppers were so shined up I could see the reflection of the doorknob in them.

"Well," I said as soon as I recovered from the shock. "How'd the job go?"

"That's what I came to tell you. It's great!"

Chalk up one satisfied customer.

"I cleaned out the cages and fed the fish and dusted the shelves," he went on, hardly pausing to take a breath, "and I didn't break a single thing."

"You didn't?" I hadn't realized that that was a major concern. If I had, I might have thought twice about siccing him on Mr. Harms.

"Just a fishbowl. A little one. But Mr. Harms said it had a chip in it so he couldn't have sold it anyway."

"That's terrific, Clinton," I said.

"Yeah." He looked as if he'd been named Business-man of the Year. "And Mr. Harms said I did so well, tomorrow he may teach me how to work the cash register." His forehead wrinkled. "I don't know about that, though."

What a change! And not just his clothes. This morning he'd never have admitted that he didn't know every single thing in the world. "The machine will do the figuring for you," I told him.

He looked relieved. "I hope it's that easy. Mr. Harms sure needs my help. He was tired. He fell asleep right in his wheelchair while I was working."

"His dog's been keeping him awake at night barking," I explained.

"At what?"

"I don't know." For a minute I considered telling Clinton about my mystery. With Cherie gone, I missed having someone my age to talk to. And now that he'd decided to drop the big macho image, at least with me, Clinton seemed more human. But I had no proof that his tendency to blab secrets had disappeared, too, and I was sure Miss Cooper wouldn't want the whole neighborhood to know about her short career as a streaker.

Even though it was obviously getting near supper-time, Clinton made no move to go home. It made me wonder if he even had one. I mean, I assumed he did, but so far he'd never mentioned his parents or brothers or sisters or other family, if he had any. In fact, I didn't know much about him at all.

"How'd you get a name like Clinton?" I asked suddenly. "I don't mean to be nosy," I added. "It's just that it isn't exactly a name you hear a lot."

"The Erie Canal."

"You were named after the Erie Canal?"

"No. My grandfather's grandfather helped dig it."

"I don't understand."

"De Witt Clinton was a man who helped get the canal built. Later he was elected governor of New York. My grandfather, whose last name was De Witt, was named after him, and I was named after my grandfather."

Once I sorted out all the De Witts and all the Clintons, it made sense. Sort of.

"I never told anyone that before," he added.

"Why not?"

"They'd think it was stupid."

"I don't. It's interesting."

"I guess you're different."

I kept thinking about Clinton long after I'd convinced him that his family might be worried if he didn't show up for supper. Maybe they wouldn't be. Maybe that was his problem. Just the small amount of encouragement I'd given him had worked wonders already. Now, if I could only figure out such an easy solution to Miss Cooper's troubles, I'd really be in business!

6

I was halfway through the funny papers the next morning by the time my mother appeared. She paused at the bottom of the stairs, waggled her fingers in a sort of greeting, yawned, and headed for the kitchen. A minute later I heard the gurgling of the coffee maker.

"How was bowling?" I asked as she came into the living room.

She was wearing a pair of gray sweatpants and a tank top. She lowered herself to the floor, where a bright patch of sunlight streaked across the carpet, and drew her bare feet up under her knees in one of the positions she'd learned in yoga class the winter before. She was always saying she needed to reduce the stress in her life, and the house was full of books like *Meditate Your Way to Health* and *Innerpeace*.

"So?" I said after a while.

"So?"

"Bowling. How was it?"

"OK." She sipped her coffee. "Do you have 'Hunt and Peck' in that section?" "Hunt and Peck," about two reporters, was her favorite comic strip.

"OK": what a terribly exciting description of a whole evening. That did it. My mother, I decided, was getting herself into a rut. And she didn't even seem to realize it. But *I* did. I didn't want to be known around town as a kid whose mother was a bag lady, even if it *was* only a bowling bag.

And speaking of ladies . . . "I saw Miss Cooper again yesterday," I said, passing her the paper.

"*Hmmm?*" She skimmed over a couple of comics, chuckling to herself. Then she said, "What? You mean the disappearing Miss Cooper?" She put the paper down. "Well, don't keep me in suspense, Penny. Was she up in another tree?"

"No. She was at the Beacon Manor Senior Citizen Residence with Mrs. Smith. She wanted to thank me for trying to help her, so she asked me over for lunch."

"And what did you find out?"

"Nothing. It was really odd, Mom. She remembered being in the tree and in our house, but that was it. She's feeling OK. She's going to stay with Mrs. Smith for a few days."

"She ought to see a doctor."

"That's what I suggested." I paused. "Mom, I liked the people I met at Beacon Manor. They're really neat. They don't act old at all."

My mother laughed. "Old is just a state of mind,

Penny. Sometimes when I wake up in the morning, I could swear I was still twenty."

Just then she didn't look much more than that, either. I wondered if she'd ever thought of putting one of those DateMate ads in the paper. "Petite, young-looking widow seeks long-term relationship with family-minded man for good times. Photo required." But did she really have to go that far? Whether she knew it or not, she had a detective in the family. And as long as I was so involved with finding jobs and finding people, why couldn't I find her a husband? I'd have to consider doing something about that when I had a little more time.

"You know," my mother went on, "I bet those people would really like it if you kept in touch. A lot of them don't have families around, and they must get pretty lonely. You could just call and say you were thinking about them and wondering how they were getting along."

And whether they were trying any more crazy stunts, like maybe skydiving, I thought to myself. I'd already made up my mind that I'd be going back to Beacon Manor. I wasn't going to get anywhere sitting around waiting for clues to come wandering by. A Girl Sleuth had to keep her nose to the trail. Or something to that effect.

Mrs. Lawler called first thing Monday and asked if I could watch Rory and Ronnie while she went out grocery shopping. She said she found it easier to just leave them at home, because when she did take them along, they ran around filling up her cart with candy and floor wax and sugar-coated cereal and motor oil and whatever else they could reach. I could believe it.

But the boys must have had a good sleep the night before. They didn't fight once and even helped me put away the dishes from the dishwasher. Half the stuff probably wouldn't surface again until a month or so later, but at least I didn't have to call the emergency squad or stop the twins from practicing mountain climbing on the bookcases.

After Mrs. Lawler got back, I remembered that my contact lens was ready to be picked up, so I headed over to the store.

Eyes Right Opticians was in a little plaza about ten blocks away. It was so nice and cool inside that I could have happily spent the rest of the day catching up on the latest issue of *People* magazine. No such luck. I hadn't even gotten past the movie reviews when I heard my name called.

A guy in a white coat with a black plastic badge that said DAVE led me to a chair in the back. I didn't see a gold band on his finger, so I started sizing him up for my mother. He wasn't bad, if you went in for the Cabbage Patch look. I didn't think my mother would be too interested.

DAVE went around behind the desk and squinted at some writing on a card. I was just going to suggest that he consider getting his eyes examined when he finished up and turned to me.

"You're here for a lens, right?"

"Yep," I said.

"Lose one?"

I started to tell him about the flour business and how I'd put my lens in the glass and everything, but halfway through the story, I saw that his attention had wandered. Someone else had come into the shop.

"Hey Bert!" DAVE yelled. "Still trying to pick up my receptionist?"

I couldn't very well turn around and stare, so I just arranged myself so I could look into the oval mirror on the desk and see into the waiting room.

Maybe it was just the reflection, but the guy seemed terribly tall. A tan cotton jacket hung easily on a set of very broad shoulders. He had jet-black, curly hair — lots of it — and though I couldn't see his face very well, I could hear his deep, husky voice.

"No, just some lens cleaner. You never bothered to tell me that Diane has a husband."

"I suppose I didn't mention his brown belt in karate, either," DAVE said.

"Terrific. I thought you said you knew some women in this town. I've been here three weeks now, and the only person I could talk into a date was Junie at the diner. Her trucker boyfriend was on a cross-country run, and she didn't want to go to the movies alone."

DAVE laughed. "I'll pick you up after work and introduce you around a few places. When word gets out, they'll be lined up a mile deep in front of the Automobile Agency."

The guy named Bert saluted and left.

I could barely sit still long enough to try on my new lens. It seemed too good to be true. A tall, dark, and handsome stranger! What could possibly be more romantic? I told DAVE the lens felt just fine. I hadn't brought the other one, though, so I popped it out again and put it back into its little plastic case. Then I put on my glasses and rushed out. I wanted to see Bert, as they say, up close and personal.

The Automobile Agency. It was in that plaza somewhere. I'd seen it a thousand times, but as always happens when you're not particularly interested in a place, you can't quite remember the exact spot.

I walked down the covered sidewalk, peering up at each sign until I rounded the corner and there it was, right in front of me.

I strolled past the place a few times, pretending to check my reflection. I was sure getting enough practice in being sneaky. But I didn't accomplish much. The sun's glare on the glass made it impossible to see a single thing inside. Frustrated, I asked myself how *Amazing Agatha* would handle this kind of situation. The answer was simple: she'd walk right in. And so, before I could talk myself out of it, that's what I did.

A long counter covered with brochures and pamphlets ran across the center of the office. Behind it I could see Bert Whatever. He was talking on the phone, with his back to me. He knew I was there, though, because he half turned and held up his hand, signaling me to wait.

Suddenly I wanted to run right back out. I was into this thing over my head. I knew that. I had absolutely no idea of what an Automobile Agency did, except that it obviously had something to do with cars. And I could hardly tell him my real reason for being there, could I?

He hung up the phone, and for the first time I got a really good look at him. He belonged on the cover of one of those flashy men's magazines. He had those dark, almost scroungy good looks that a lot of movie actors go in for these days — on the verge of needing a shave, except that would have utterly destroyed the effect. The top button of his shirt was open and his tie hung off to one side a bit. And when he smiled, as he was doing now —

"What can I do for you, young lady?"

I could only stare at him while my mind furiously tried to glue one or two intelligent thoughts together. Agatha Potts, I was sure, would have had this all planned out ahead of time. Fortunately, before it could get too embarrassing, I spied a poster on the wall over his left shoulder: *Ask about Our Travel Planning Service*. I was saved.

"My m-mother and I are th-thinking of taking our vacation in . . . uh, in Colorado. In the mountains," I added, because that was the first thing I remembered about Colorado.

"I see. Did you have any specific ideas about what sorts of activities you'd be interested in?"

Activities? "Skiing?" I suggested, because that was the second thing I remembered about Colorado.

His smile showed a set of slightly crooked but very white teeth. "And when were you expecting to go, Miss —" He paused.

"Potts," I replied quickly. (Detectives sometimes have to use sudo . . . psudo . . . fake names.) "We'll probably be going sometime next month."

"August?"

I started to nod, then realized what I'd said. My face grew hot. "I mean next *winter*, of course," I said quickly.

Ten minutes later I was holding a bunch of papers (including an application form for membership), a map of the Midwest, a business card, and a free compass key chain. Then I was out the door. Oh, I also knew as much as I'd ever need to about emergency road service, the Automobile Agency's certified driving school, and its low insurance rates.

The thing was, I hadn't found out a single interesting fact about — what *was* his name, anyway? I read the card. ROBERT REYNOLDS. SERVICE REPRESENTATIVE. Robert Reynolds. Respectable enough — only DAVE at Eyes Right had called him something else. Bert.

I took a few steps before it sank in. Bert Reynolds. Was he serious? Talk about cutesy! Oh well, maybe it meant the guy had a sense of humor. I'd done the groundwork. Now I could leave it to my mother to get all the juicy details, such as whether he had an ex-wife and three kids stashed away someplace. When and if I could get the two of them together, that was.

The opportunity came up sooner than I'd expected.

I'd just unlocked the front door and headed into the kitchen for a glass of cold milk when my mother called to ask if I'd picked up my lens.

"I can get it for you on the way home," she said.

I told her I'd already done it, then rushed on, "But you can do me another favor."

"Sure. What is it?"

With the exception of the ski trip to Colorado in August, I wasn't doing too badly at inventing stories on the spot. If I didn't make it as a detective, maybe I could become a writer after all. "Cherie keeps sending me all these postcards," I said. "I don't want to throw them out. I thought about hanging them up in my room, but wouldn't it be neat if I had a map and could run arrows or something to show where they came from? Sort of a geography mural." Parents would agree to almost anything if you made it sound educational.

She waited for me to get to the point.

"I think they have maps at the Automobile Agency in the plaza." I held my breath.

"No trouble. I'm going right by there. See you at about five-thirty."

I checked the clock on the stove. Four-thirty. A whole hour of suspense. I dove into the refrigerator, dragged out all the leftovers from the weekend and started to put a supper together. The lettuce had seen better days, but I tore off the brown spots, added an onion, half a tomato, and some grated cheese and bacon pieces. Then I looked at the small package of ground beef.

I know there are at least five hundred ways to fix hamburger, but I could only think of one. I cooked the stuff, threw in some pasta spirals and a cup or so of spaghetti sauce, and let it simmer. In no time, it seemed, I heard my mother coming in the door.

"Did you get the map?" I asked before she could even hang up her keys.

"Uh-huh. It's here in my purse somewhere. And I met the nicest man, too."

"Man?" I asked.

"Ok, *guy*, then." She grinned. "He found the map for me and we talked for a bit. He asked me for my phone number."

All right! "Does he have a name?" I asked, casually.

"Dave."

Dave? Eyes Right DAVE? What was he doing, moon-lighting?

I turned my back so she couldn't see my face. "That's . . . uh, nice," I said, with a silent groan. Just my luck I'd end up with a Cabbage Patch stepfather!

It was Tuesday before I got hold of Miss Cooper. I tried calling Beacon Manor, but Lydia Smith told me she'd already gone back home to Wellington Place.

"I'd have felt much more comfortable if she'd stayed here," Lydia told me. "But Miss Bitterman said that we couldn't start taking in permanent boarders, and that Katherine would have to put her name on the waiting list. Several of us tried to talk her into that, of course, but Katherine wouldn't hear of it. She intends to keep on living by herself. I suppose the next thing we know, we'll find her flying a hot-air balloon across the ocean, and it won't be quite so easy to get her down again. Shall I tell her you called?"

"I'd like to talk to her," I said. "Do you think she'd mind if you gave me her phone number?"

"Not at all. She was just mentioning you yesterday. She said she'd almost forgotten what a joy it was to be around young people again, and that meeting you was better than any medicine a doctor could order."

It sounded very much as though Miss Cooper wasn't about to get herself a checkup.

She answered on the third ring. "Why, Penny! How delightful. I was just about to call you myself and let you know I was back home. You'll have to come to dinner sometime."

"Sure," I said. "You're feeling OK, then?"

"I certainly am. Perhaps it was just one of those odd occurrences." A bit of an understatement, I'd say. "I realize I'm getting along in age," she went on, "but I've kept my mind too active for it to desert me now."

I wondered if she really believed everything she was telling me. I didn't think so. Underneath all that "life must go on" stuff, she still sounded a little nervous. I didn't want her to give up on finding out what had happened — mostly for herself, but partly for me, too. So far I hadn't gotten to do much real detecting. Now it looked like my first big case was going to just fade out on me.

"What does Lydia — I mean, what does Mrs. Smith say?" I asked.

"Oh, Lydia is quite adamant about my signing up for an apartment at Beacon Manor," Miss Cooper replied. "That was all she could talk about at the bridge table yesterday. At first Edward tried to convince me to stay, too. But finally he said that if I was going to insist on living on my own, the least I could do would be to take in a roomer. I've been considering it."

I had to agree with Mr. Netterich. Even Mr. Harms wasn't completely alone. He had Barney, at least.

"A dog!" I shouted into the receiver. There was silence on the other end. For a minute I was afraid I had burst her eardrums.

Then she spoke. "A dog?"

"Uh, well, I was just thinking that maybe you could get some kind of a pet. Something to keep you company. It wouldn't necessarily have to be a dog. A canary, maybe."

"What an unusual idea," she murmured. "Although I *have* read that pets make excellent companions for the elderly. One wouldn't have to be concerned about sharing the hot water or television programs. But not a bird. I can't abide fluttery things. No, I think your first suggestion was a good one. I used to have a dog when I was young. However, I couldn't handle anything too large. I can't imagine being dragged down the street by some behemoth."

(BEHEMOTH: *noun*: a huge or powerful animal.)

"Do you happen to know the name of a reliable pet store?" she asked.

Did I ever!

71

7

I was wiping off the kitchen counter after supper that night when I noticed Mr. Harms out watering his flowers. I'd promised Miss Cooper that I'd check with him as soon as I could about getting her a dog. I turned on the dishwasher, emptied the glop from the metal drain stopper into the garbage, and went out back.

"Hi, Mr. Harms," I called.

"Hello there, Penny." He turned off the nozzle and steered over to the fence. "You know, that young lad you brought over the other day is doing just fine. Got a real gentle touch. The animals seem to like him."

I was glad to hear Clinton was a hit with the gerbil set.

"He's a mite clumsy, though." Mr. Harms chuckled. "Dropped a five-pound bag of birdseed behind the counter today. But he used his head. Swept it up, put it back in the bag, and then sold it for half price to a customer for a wedding. Seems they throw bird seed instead of rice or confetti these days. No mess."

I made a note of that on the off chance that I could invent some other excuse to get my mother into the Automobile Agency — this time without DAVE around to louse things up.

"Mr. Harms, there's a woman I know who wants to buy a dog. Do you have any at the shop?"

"She in a hurry?"

I shrugged, but it suddenly occurred to me that when you were getting up in years, you might not want to spend an awful lot of time waiting around for things to happen, so I told him she was.

"Well then, I do have a couple coming in. Let me think. Might be tomorrow. A Chihuahua for certain, and maybe a Lhasa apso."

I pictured a dog carrying bales of cotton down the sides of the Andes mountains.

"You tell your friend that if she's interested she should stop by on Thursday afternoon to take a look," Mr. Harms said.

"I will, Mr. Harms. And thanks!"

You could tell Clinton really loved working at the Green Lizard. The place was spotless. The fish tanks gleamed. A bunch of green and blue parakeets squawked at the tops of their lungs in a freshly lined birdcage, and all the shelves were stocked and neat. In the front window he'd made a sort of jungle for Tico-Tico, the iguana, with some big-leafed plants that drooped over a small plastic pool. Tico-Tico was blissfully asleep in the sun on a large piece of slate, his tail hanging down into the water.

Clinton blended right into the scenery. He had on a Hawaiian shirt splashed all over with palm trees and surfboards. He was a walking travel poster. Obviously Clinton didn't just *wear* clothes; he used them to make announcements.

"What time is this lady coming?" he asked, for the third time in fifteen minutes.

"Around four-thirty," I answered, also for the third time in fifteen minutes. "Relax, Clinton. She's just going to buy a dog, not check to see if you left any spider webs under the shelves."

"Did I?" He looked panicky.

I sighed. Clinton was already pretty shaky over the possibility of having to ring up such a big sale with tax and all on the cash register. If Miss Cooper didn't show up soon, he was going to disintegrate right in front of me.

Miss Cooper was supposed to be driving over with Mrs. Smith. "I had quite a time talking Lydia into it," she'd told me over the phone that morning. "She says I'm being extremely foolish and insists I move into Beacon Manor. I said the only way I would leave my own home would be if I were carried out, feet first."

That hot potato must have gone back and forth a few times in the past week.

The clock on the wall behind the counter said a quarter to five. I didn't want to admit it to Clinton, but

I was getting worried, too. What if Miss Cooper had had another spell and was stuck up in a tree again, only this time in front of City Hall?

I wandered into the back room, where the larger animal cages were kept. Mr. Harms was at a worktable, slowly filling bowls with dry puppy food from a huge bag beside him.

Four of the six cages were occupied. In one of the bigger ones was a beautiful silvery-white Siberian husky with bright-blue eyes. I almost couldn't find the Chihuahua. He was rolled up in a ball behind a squeaky toy, but when I came near him, he started a high-pitched yipping. That woke up the beagle next door and an animated dust mop in the cage below. It had caramel-colored fur, two beady eyes, and a row of scraggly bottom teeth that reminded me of the piranhas' in the fish tank behind the counter.

The bell over the door jangled. I went out front and found Miss Cooper. She was alone. She seemed distracted, but she was in one piece and so were her clothes, so I figured if she'd had any more problems, they couldn't have been as terrible as before.

"Lydia wasn't available," she informed me. "I had to take the public transportation."

The bus, I translated.

"I was waiting for her," she went on, "but then she called and said she couldn't make it. Alice Pringle has developed some strange malady and won't let anyone but Lydia near her."

(MALADY: *noun*: illness.)

I remembered Alice. She was the hitchhiker who had nearly kidnapped me at Beacon Manor. "That's too bad," I said.

"Isn't it. She's a kind woman, and I imagine she's quite frightened by this new situation. Lydia says that whenever anyone goes near Alice, they get an electric shock. I've never heard of such a thing. However, there are so few surprises left in this world, I should be grateful when I discover one. In any case, I'm here. Let's get on with it."

"Great," I said. "By the way, Miss Cooper, this is my friend Clinton. He's Mr. Harms' assistant."

Clinton put on his best salesman's expression. Miss Cooper, however, just stared at him curiously.

"I've seen you before," she murmured half out loud.

Clinton looked puzzled.

"This is the fastest way to go to the dogs," I broke in with my usual cleverness. Why did Miss Cooper have to pick right now to start remembering things? I steered her into the back room. Clinton wandered along, too.

Mr. Harms was putting the last bowl into the Chihuahua's cage. The Chihuahua was so excited he was bouncing off the walls. He hit the wire door, which came down with a *clang* right on Mr. Harms' fingers. Mr. Harms let out a couple of words that I recognized, but not because I'd seen them in a dictionary.

I could hear Miss Cooper's sharp intake of breath, but she didn't say anything. She marched stiffly up to the cage, where the Chihuahua was now really into his dinner. In fact, he was sitting right in the dish. "What," she asked "is that rat doing in here?"

"It's not a rat," Clinton replied, eager to show off his new knowledge. "It's a Chihuahua. It's not going to get much bigger, either. Mr. Harms says people used to carry them around in their pockets."

"I said Xavier Cugat did," grumbled Mr. Harms. Noticing Miss Cooper's rather blank look, he went on. "The bandleader?"

She shook her head.

"I used to rumba way past the time the cows came home. Half the time, the rooster'd been long up, too." He tried to snap his fingers, then frowned. "Dammit. First the legs go, then you can't even do anything with your hands."

Miss Cooper winced. Then she asked, "May we get back to business, young man?"

I thought for a minute that she was talking to Clinton, but then I noticed she was looking straight at Mr. Harms. Young man? I considered both of them — well — old. When I thought about it, though, I remembered my mother's saying that Mr. Harms was only in his late sixties. According to Lydia Smith, Miss Cooper was eighty-two. That meant there was better than ten years' difference in their ages — which was a whole lot more than the six between me and the Lawler twins, and they seemed like babies!

Mr. Harms grimaced, then opened the dust mop's cage, took him out, and plopped him in Miss Cooper's arms before she could even set her purse down. "This

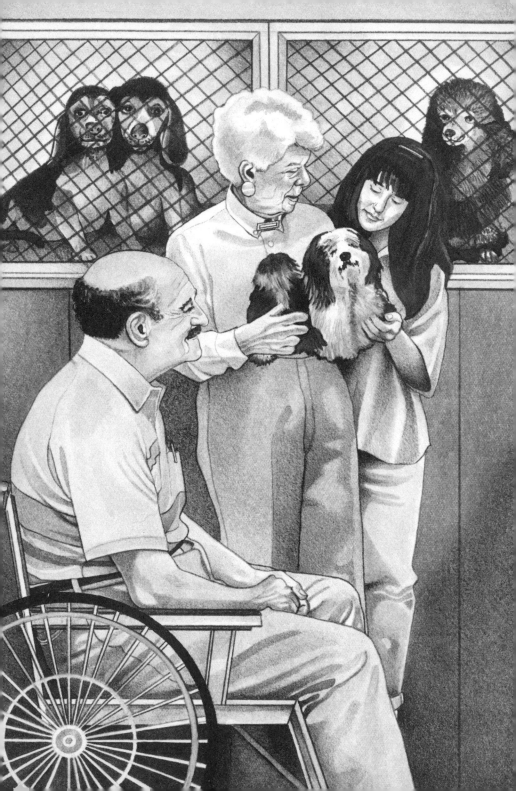

here's a Lhasa apso. The only way you're going to know if this is your style of animal is to get acquainted. Now go sit down in that there chair and see how you like each other." He pointed to an old wooden rocker over in the corner.

Surprisingly, she did just what he'd said. The Lhasa tried to lick her face a couple of times, but she held him back with a firm yet gentle grip and he settled down. Only when they'd both been quiet for several minutes did she dare look up. "Animals can teach us a great deal about affection and simple courtesy," she said, smiling at Mr. Harms. But her words had a crisp edge to them.

Whoops! I thought. Maybe I hadn't done such a great thing in bringing these two together. They were both really nice people. I couldn't understand why they were irritating one another.

"*Harumph!*" Mr. Harms cleared his throat. "Penny, I got so many aches in my joints today that I think it'd be best if I went on home and let your friend here make up her own mind. She seems to have a pretty firm idea of what she likes and what she don't." He was rubbing his knuckles. They were twice their usual size. He seemed to be having trouble even operating the controls of his wheelchair.

"That is a sensible suggestion," Miss Cooper said. "At any rate, I wouldn't be able to take an animal back with me today." She pulled a slip of paper from the front pocket of her purse and consulted it. "My bus will be coming at five-thirty. That should give me plenty of time to make my selection."

Mr. Harms grunted. "Clinton, you take these keys. When it's time to close up, count the money and put it in the safe. You can drop the keys in my mailbox on your way home."

I'd never seen him so gruff before, and I was worried. He was really in pain. "Let me go with you," I offered.

"I can handle myself just fine," he said.

Over in the rocker, Miss Cooper sniffed. "A strong man knows when to accept help."

"Please," I said. Then, so he'd feel better about it, I added, "We could always drag race a few cars on the way."

I got Mr. Harms home and let Barney go out back for a few minutes. Mr. Harms told me where to find his arthritis medicine in the bathroom cabinet, and I wrestled with the kiddie-proof top for ten minutes before I got it off. I wondered how he managed, even when his hands weren't so swollen.

I popped in a microwave dinner. When it was done, I put it on a tray in the living room and left Mr. Harms in his easy chair watching TV, with the remote within easy reach. Then I went across the lawn to my own house.

On the kitchen table I found another postcard from Cherie, along with a note from my mother that said she was going to the movies. She didn't say who with, and I figured it was probably DAVE. I picked up Cherie's card.

It was the standard "having a wonderful time" junk,

except where she wrote that she'd visited the College of William and Mary and couldn't wait to finish high school. She didn't have to tell me what she was going to study. Cherie had recently discovered a very interesting homophone for the word *mail.* "What's new?" she'd scribbled at the bottom. "Nothing," I muttered to myself, suddenly realizing how much I missed her, "except finding a naked lady in a tree."

I made myself a cup of instant soup, shuffled through the newspapers and junk on the coffee table until I unearthed my new book, *Agent Agatha,* and curled up on the couch. My mother found me there, asleep, and made me go up to bed.

Ping!

Something bounced off the screen of my bedroom window. The sky was light and the birds were already serving breakfast to their families in the trees outside. I stayed very still and waited.

Ping!

Somebody was trying to get my attention. I made it to the window just as a fairly large rock tore a hole in the screen and dropped over the sill and onto my bare foot.

"*Ouch!*" I peered out. "Clinton! What on earth —"

"Penny, you've got to help me. I'm dead meat!" He was jumping up and down on the grass.

"What's the matter?"

"I locked her up. I forgot. I *knew* I was going to do that. I'm just no good. You've got to come."

"Locked *who* up?"

"The lady. The one who wanted the dog."

"Miss Cooper? You — Clinton, tell me you didn't leave her in the Lizard."

"I'd like to, Penny, but —"

"I'll be right down."

I threw my clothes on so fast it was two hours later before I realized I had on orange shorts, a red T-shirt, and no socks. I also grabbed my old glasses with the safety pin holding them together. This was no time to be messing around with contacts.

Clinton met me at the front door. "Hurry!" he begged. "I took the key out of Mr. Harms's mailbox. Maybe if we get there real fast, he won't know what I did."

We raced down Tucker Street. "I don't believe this," I panted. "I just can't believe you'd lock an old woman in a store all night."

I could see the sweat dripping down his face and neck, staining the front of his shirt. "She was holding the dog. I don't know what happened. It was so quiet, I guess I just forgot about her. When it got to be six o'clock, I did what Mr. Harms told me to do. I put the money in the safe and locked the door. I had a funny feeling something was wrong, but you're always telling me to stop worrying, so I did."

The Green Lizard was in sight now. The dark shade on the front window was down. Everything seemed quiet.

Clinton's hands were shaking so hard he couldn't even get the key into the lock. I grabbed it away from him and opened the door.

There wasn't a sound in the whole place, except for the occasional ruffle of parakeet feathers.

"Miss Cooper?" I called softly.

The little Lhasa apso appeared from the back room. He scrunched down on the floor, stretching his back legs behind him. His little tail waved a cheery greeting.

I tiptoed across the floor. Miss Cooper was sitting in the chair, exactly where she'd been when I left. I listened. There was a faint snore. Clinton grabbed my shoulder and almost sent me through the ceiling.

The Lhasa ran over to Miss Cooper and tried to jump up into her lap.

"*Mmmmm?*" Her eyes opened. "Why, Penny! Is it five-thirty? I must catch my bus." She yawned. "I think I dropped off for a moment. I was having the strangest dream. I was in a restaurant, having a fish dinner. It was the most delicious meal, and I kept ordering plate after plate."

I took a step toward her, skidded on a large puddle of water, and nearly killed myself trying to keep from falling on my back. I stared at the water, then at the Lhasa. He looked pretty innocent. I looked back at the puddle. There were strands of green aquatic plants floating around in it. This was really weird. How could such a mess have gotten there? As insecure as Clinton seemed at times, I knew he'd never leave the store in such a terrible condition.

Then I looked at Clinton. His eyes were focused straight ahead, glued on the side wall, where several freshwater fish tanks were lined up. The day before, they'd been filled with guppies and goldfish and black mollies and zebras and a bunch of other kinds. Now every one of the tanks was, except for the rest of the water and green plants, completely empty.

Behind me, Miss Cooper burped.

8

Her face went just a shade or two lighter than Tico-Tico. She didn't utter a word, but an unspoken question hung in the air.

Even if I wasn't Agatha Potts, I knew what the answer had to be. Incredible though it seemed, there just wasn't any other explanation for the empty tanks. Especially now that I could see the line of damp footprints crossing the floor. From the first minute I'd laid eyes on Miss Cooper in the Mendelsohns' maple, things had kept getting more and more bewildering. And now this. Lydia Smith had been right. Something strange was happening to Miss Cooper. Something very strange indeed.

What was I going to do? I couldn't very well stick her on a bus and let her find her own way home. And I sure didn't want her staying at the Lizard, staring at all those floating plants. I had to get her someplace where she'd feel safe and where I could decide on my next move.

I was tired of playing detective. My brain hurt. Maybe Miss Cooper *was* getting senile and preferred Meals on Waves to Meals on Wheels. Maybe she *did* belong at Beacon Manor, where there'd be someone to keep an eye on her. I glanced over at Clinton. His head was buried in his arms on top of the counter. He was probably wishing he was standing guard at some forsaken army base in Alaska. Well, he wasn't the only one.

However, as one losing football coach or another always seems to be quoted as saying, when the going gets tough, the tough get going. It was time for action.

"Stand up, Clinton!" I ordered.

He couldn't help it. There was still a lot of soldier left inside him. His back automatically became a straight line, and his chest thrust forward. I think if I'd yelled "March!" just then, he'd have tramped right out the door without giving it a thought. But I didn't need his mind — just his muscles.

"Take her other arm," I told him. "We're going to my house."

She didn't offer any resistance. "It's a beautiful morning," I said soothingly. "Just take it nice and slow."

She burped again, and I could smell a faint fishy odor.

I felt like a walking ambulance as I steered Clinton and Miss Cooper down Tenth Avenue and up Tucker Street. The few people who were out that early weren't awake enough to pay much attention to us. I kept babbling away about how dry the gardens were getting and how we could probably use a good rain again and stuff like that to keep my passengers moving. We were almost home — right opposite the Mendelsohns' maple, in fact — when I saw the van in our driveway. A man was backing out our front door with a picnic basket in one hand and a beach umbrella tucked under his arm. It was Bert Reynolds!

I ducked my head quickly. I couldn't believe my mother. She was turning into a regular Dating Game contestant. I'd thought she was busy enough with Cabbage Patch DAVE. How had she come up with Bert Reynolds, too? I mean, sure, it was just what I'd been scheming for, but did she have to do it just then? That was one complication I didn't need, especially with Clinton and Miss Cooper on my hands. Literally. No, home was definitely not the best place to be right at the moment. But where?

The answer was simple, once I calmed down. Mr. Harms lived next door. To him Miss Cooper was just another customer, not some weird old lady who went around climbing trees in her birthday suit. I was sure he'd let us in if I made up some kind of explanation. I wouldn't necessarily have to go into all the details about what had happened at the store, would I?

I felt like an international spy as I slinked past Bert Reynolds and up Mr. Harms' driveway to the ramp at his back door. Barney came sniffing at the screen, then let out a low growl.

"It's OK, boy," I said soothingly. He wagged his tail

at my familiar voice, but his ears kept lying back and then standing up as if he wasn't quite sure if we were supposed to be there.

"Who is it?" Mr. Harms shuffled toward the door, peering over the top of a pair of funny-looking half glasses.

"It's me, Mr. Harms," I said. "Penny. I'm with Clinton and Miss Cooper. We need to use your phone."

He grunted and made some comment about being surprised to find a convention on his doorstep at this hour, but he came and unhooked the latch.

"Down." He placed his hand gently on the dog's back and shooed him out into the yard as we entered. Seeing Miss Cooper's rather glazed expression, Mr. Harms whispered, "What's the matter with her?"

"It's a long story," I said evasively.

Once inside, Miss Cooper seemed more like her old self — I mean, the way she was before she wiped out the tanks. She wandered around the kitchen, eyeing the counter, where there was a small pile of dirty dishes. "I've read that soaking one's hands in dishwater will help keep them supple," was her first announcement.

(SUPPLE: *adjective*: flexible.)

She obviously remembered enough about Mr. Harms to know how to annoy him. The top of his head blushed. "I wasn't fishing for any home remedies," he said.

At the mention of the word *fish,* Miss Cooper let out a small "Oh," did another iguana imitation, and sat down on the nearest chair. Her green face and Mr. Harms' red one made me think of Christmas decorations.

"Miss Cooper has to call for a ride home," I put in before Mr. Harms could start asking embarrassing questions. "She came too early. She wanted to take another look at the dog and forgot that you only have afternoon hours during the week." Not bad, I thought to myself. I was steadily improving my creativity. No more used-car ads for Penny Eagan!

I glanced over at Miss Cooper, hoping she'd help me out with my explanation, but she was busy trying to rub off a few water spots from her jacket.

"Clinton said we could get the key out of your mailbox," I continued, "but I — Clinton?"

Clinton had been edging toward the door. I caught up with him just as he reached it. "Clinton, you can't leave now," I whispered desperately.

"I don't understand what's going on, Penny," he whined. "You don't need me. All I do is mess things up."

I was tired of his sniveling. "*Behemoth!*" I muttered under my breath. Then, out loud, I said, "Maybe so, but I didn't think you were a quitter. I have to get Miss Cooper back home somehow. I need help, and you're it. Got it?"

"I —"

"Good." I turned on my heel and walked back into the kitchen. After a minute or two Clinton followed.

Mr. Harms was explaining to Miss Cooper that he

had to get something into his stomach before his ulcer started acting up. He dug into a bowl of what looked like Barney's dog kibble. One of those high-fiber cereals, I guessed. Miss Cooper just kept bobbing her head up and down. Then suddenly she spoke.

"Thank you for showing me your store," she said to Mr. Harms. "I'm sorry I put you to all that trouble. I'm afraid I won't be getting a dog after all."

"Why not?" he asked.

She hesitated while she covered another small burp with her hand. "I can't be alone. I've decided it's best that I move to Beacon Manor."

"No!" I cried, completely forgetting I'd just been thinking the same thing. "You *can't!*"

"Why would you want to go and do a foolish thing like that when you have a place of your own?" Mr. Harms dropped his spoon into the empty bowl with a clatter. "You seem perfectly healthy to me."

I wondered if he'd have the same opinion if he knew she'd wiped out a generation or two of his guppy stock. "You *like* living by yourself," I broke in. "You don't want to hang around with a bunch of *old* people!" I stopped as I realized what I'd said.

"She has a point," Mr. Harms said with a grin.

"But *I* am old," Miss Cooper said firmly.

"Suit yourself. I'm glad I ain't." Mr. Harms put his hands on the table and pushed himself to his feet. He picked up his cereal bowl and made his way slowly over to the sink.

"Not," corrected Miss Cooper, instinctively.

"Huh?"

"I'm glad I'm *not*."

"You just said you were. Can't you even make up your mind?"

These two needed a referee. My mother was right. People didn't change a heck of a lot just because they'd blown out a few more birthday candles. Miss Cooper and Mr. Harms were just an old-fashioned version of Ronnie and Rory Lawler.

"Perhaps I've painted too bleak a picture of Beacon Manor," Miss Cooper said. "It's really quite a lovely place. The grounds are spacious and well cared for, and one can have company or not simply by the judicious use of one's door."

(JUDICIOUS: *adjective*: appropriate, wise.)

"You can't grow your own roses, I bet," put in Mr. Harms.

"I think not, but I do know that they encourage residents to help out with the flower beds around the building, if they wish."

"*Hmm*." Mr. Harms looked thoughtful. "Maybe I ought to go check the place out. You never can tell but that I might end up there myself if my legs get worse."

"I'm afraid that would be impossible," said Miss Cooper. "You must be able to perambulate."

"What's that mean?"

I was glad I wasn't the only one who had to translate Miss Cooper.

"It means that you must be able to get around on your own," she replied.

"How come?"

"Safety regulations. But there is a very active Senior Citizens' Club that meets there daily. Perhaps you should consider joining it. You might enjoy playing bridge."

"Bridge!" Mr. Harms snorted. "Sissy game. Ain't you ever heard of poker?"

"I have heard of it, certainly," she said. "I'm sure some of the men indulge from time to time."

"If you want, I could teach it to you," he offered.

She shuddered slightly but only said, "Perhaps." Then she said, "Why don't you come along with us?"

"Now?"

"Yes. I was just about to call my friend Lydia for a ride home. I know she'd be delighted to show you Beacon Manor. Of course, she thinks it's Buckingham Palace and the Taj Mahal in one. Penny, you and your friend are quite welcome to come along. And while we're there, I could phone Dr. Melrose for an appointment regarding these little lapses of memory I've been having lately."

I had to hand it to her. Next she'd be calling a hurricane a breeze. But she was obviously determined to sweep this latest incident under the rug, at least as far as Mr. Harms was concerned.

"Aw, don't let them things bother you none," Mr. Harms said. "I figure as long as you know your own name and remember to put your pants on in the morning —"

"Let's call Mrs. Smith now," I interrupted.

I stepped over to the counter, picked up the telephone directory, and began looking up Beacon Manor's number. A beep from next door interrupted my search. I looked out and saw Bert Reynolds behind the wheel of the van and my mother in the doorway shaking her head. Bert got out, and then they both went back inside the house.

Suddenly I realized she was probably looking for me. I'd gone out too quickly to think of leaving a note or anything.

"I have to go home for a minute," I said quickly. "I'll be right back. Clinton, take charge." He hustled over. "Call this number." I pointed it out to him. "Ask for Lydia Smith, and tell her Miss Cooper needs a ride. Tell her she's at my house. That's close enough."

I hurried out the back door and hopped the fence. There was an old wooden trellis with nothing growing on it in the corner where the garage hooked on to my house. I'd tried it out once. I'd never planned on using it as anything other than an emergency escape route, at least until I was old enough to really need it. But this sure qualified as an emergency as far as I was concerned, even if I was trying to get *in*, not out. My mother was going to have cops crawling all over Tucker Street if I didn't surface soon.

I made it up to the garage roof, only to find my way blocked by the screen on my window. I'd forgotten about its being summer. Then I remembered the hole that Clinton's rock had made that morning. Balancing myself on one foot, I reached over, stuck my hand inside, unhooked the latch, and pulled the screen far enough out so I could swing my leg over the sill. I was inside.

I stole over to the door and opened it a crack.

"I won't step one foot out of this door until I know where my daughter is," my mother was saying.

"Come on, Barb. Didn't you tell me you've had to leave her alone a lot? She's got to be a pretty resourceful kid by now."

Mr. Reynolds, I presumed.

"There's such a thing as being *too* resourceful," my mother replied. "She's only thirteen. Look, why don't you go ahead and get us a good spot? As soon as I find Penny, the two of us will drive over."

The two of us? Great.

As soon as I heard the van's engine, I walked down the stairs.

"Penny!" My mother stared at me. "Where have you been?"

I started to say something, but then the front door opened. "Barb, I forgot to tell you I'm going to be at the Braeside section of the —" Bert Reynolds stopped. "Well, good *morning* . . . uh, Miss Potts, was it? Nice to see you again."

"Potts?" said my mother.

I sank down on the steps.

There was a pounding at the side door. "Penny? It's Clinton. Are you in there? That Lydia lady says somebody borrowed her car and she can't come. Barney has Miss Cooper trapped in a corner of the kitchen and she swatted him on the nose and —"

"Cooper?" asked my mother.

"I've changed my mind about going out to the park," Bert Reynolds said, pocketing his car keys. "Somehow I feel this is going to be much more interesting than a picnic."

9

Clinton kept on pounding on the door and yelling, while my mother just stood there in one of those classic poses that teenagers see an average of once a day. It was all Bert Reynolds could do to keep from coming completely unglued. The smirk on his face grew bigger every minute. Why had I ever told him my name was Potts? I guess I'd gotten too wrapped up in playing detective. I know it sounds sort of dumb, but just then I wished the ground would open up under my feet. Of course it didn't, and it appeared as if Bert Reynolds was my only hope.

"Mr. Reynolds," I began desperately, "Clinton and I have to go somewhere with some friends of ours. They're old, and they don't have a car. Could you possibly give us a ride in your van?" It just about killed me to ask.

He grinned maddeningly. "Certainly, Miss *Potts*. My limo's at your disposal."

My mother just kept looking blank.

"Grab your tennis racquet, Barb," he said. "We should be able to wrap this up in short order and then get on with the day."

In no time, it seemed, I'd settled Clinton down, helped Mr. Harms shut Barney up in the bathroom, and maneuvered everybody aboard the van, and we were off.

It was pretty awkward. My mother had never met Clinton, Miss Cooper had never met my mother, and Bert Reynolds was a complete stranger to just about everybody. I tried to make introductions. Needless to say, it was pretty tricky, especially with Bert and my mother in the front seat with their backs to us. I could just imagine what was going on in everyone's head. My mother knew about Miss Cooper's being in the tree, though Miss Cooper didn't know that she knew. Three of us were keeping very quiet about the disappearance of a tankful of guppies. Mr. Harms was the only one who was enjoying himself, looking out the window completely oblivious to the fact that there was something odd about this whole trip.

What we had in that van was one of those big, long scientific equations that cover both sides of six sheets of paper and never reach a conclusion that anyone can understand.

Nobody spoke for a full fifteen minutes. Then we pulled up the circular drive at the Beacon Manor Senior Citizen Residence. The people on the front porch must have thought they were at a circus, watching all the clowns pile out. Bert Reynolds got the wheelchair down and helped Mr. Harms into it. Clinton watched him and then, surprisingly, offered his arm to Miss Cooper, who, also surprisingly, took it. My mother and I climbed out by ourselves.

Miss Cooper seemed a bit more composed now that she was in familiar territory and didn't have to live in mortal fear of becoming Barney's next helping of Alpo.

"There's a ramp on the other side of the porch," she told Mr. Harms. She started off in that direction. Mr. Harms turned his chair on and followed, with Clinton only a step or two behind. I wasn't quite sure what to do. I didn't want to leave. Even if Miss Cooper was ready to give up, I wasn't. I hadn't the foggiest idea of why she'd been up in the Mendelsohns' maple or what had really happened at the Green Lizard, though I now had a funny feeling I was getting closer to some answers. On the other hand, I couldn't expect my mother to just drive off, either.

She surprised me, though. "I suppose it would be a shame not to take advantage of this beautiful sun," she said to Bert Reynolds. "Not that I'm excusing you from an explanation, young lady, but this happens to be the only day I have off this week. We'll talk later." She winked at me. I guess she thought I wouldn't get into any trouble in a senior citizens' home. Little did she know.

"I thought you said the guy you met at the Automobile Agency was named Dave," I said to her as Bert walked around to the other side of the van.

"That's right. I must have forgotten to mention that when I met him, he was just holding down the fort for his friend. Dave already has a steady girlfriend, but he thought Bert might be interested in meeting me. I suspect you're quite familiar with that kind of scheming."

I bit my lip.

She opened the van door and climbed up.

"See you later, Potts," Bert called as he put the van in gear.

I didn't know what to make of Bert Reynolds. There wasn't any doubt that both he and my mother knew I'd been playing cupid. But at least he wasn't making too big a deal out of it. I just hoped he appreciated the favor I'd done for him. He wouldn't have to worry about Junie or her trucker boyfriend anymore.

There seemed to be a bit of a commotion at the front desk when I finally got there. Jessica Bitterman was insisting that she couldn't authorize so many visitors. Miss Cooper was a legitimate member of the Senior Citizens' Club, of course, but the manager wasn't sure about the rest of us. It could have been Mr. Harms' wheelchair, or maybe my orange shorts, red shirt, and no socks. Then Mr. Harms said he was looking into joining the club, so eventually she gave in and said we could all stay, provided we signed the register.

"Bunch of bureaucratic red tape," I heard Mr. Harms mumble as we headed down the hall.

Miss Cooper stopped in front of a set of double

doors. "This is the Recreation Room," she said. "It's where we play cards. I'll just see if Lydia is here. You may come in, if you like."

Mr. Harms switched off the power on his wheelchair and used his hands to steer himself. Clinton and I brought up the rear.

The room was like a regular family room, only bigger. At one end it had a pool table, which no one was using at the moment. Two ladies sat on a sofa, quietly doing needlework.

"Down two doubled! Ha!"

I recognized the voice. It was Edward Netterich, the man I'd met on my last trip. He was seated at a card table with three others. To his left was Lydia Smith, and next to her was a rather petite woman with a pleased expression on her face. But it was the fourth member of the game who caught my attention. She had risen to her feet, and if there was ever a perfect definition of the word *bizarre,* she was it.

Her hair was long and black and looked like it hadn't seen a comb in twenty years. She was wearing a fiery red blouse that was gathered around the neckline and had huge, puffy sleeves down to her wrists. Strings of beads of every color and size were draped around her neck, along with an enormous round gold pendant that hung in the center. Big gold hoops dangled from her ears, and her jet-black eyes flashed angrily around the table before settling on Edward Netterich.

"You do not open," she said with a heavy accent.

"You have more zan enough points, but you do not open."

"No," Mr. Netterich said cheerily. "We had a much better defensive hand, didn't we, Marion?"

The woman across the table nodded.

"But you must open with zixteen points!" You *must!*"

"Ordinarily, I would agree. But there's nothing to say what I did was illegal. That's why bridge is so interesting. If I remember correctly, Kitty tripped you up the same way a few weeks ago. I hardly think we should be sentenced to being boiled in oil just because you can't communicate your cards properly, Anna."

"It is Madame Krevotsky to you, zir!" The wild-looking woman grabbed at her beads and rattled them fiercely.

Mr. Netterich bowed. "Excuse *me*, Madame. And I am Edward, Duke of Disaster."

A muffled laugh escaped from Lydia Smith before she clamped her hand over her mouth.

Madame Krevotsky's anger seemed to turn instantly to ice. She stared at Mr. Netterich so hard I thought her eyes would bore holes through his head. "Zo, you have ze fun with me, no?" she hissed. "Do you know what I think? I think you are nossing more zan an old goat!" With that, she turned sharply and stalked away from the table. She didn't seem to notice the rest of us as she brushed past and was gone. I could've sworn I could hear the clatter of her beads even after the door had closed behind her.

"*Well,*" said Miss Cooper.

"Katherine!" cried Lydia Smith. "Then you did get a ride after all. I felt terrible, but there was nothing I could do. The Overholts needed to do some grocery shopping this morning, and their car wouldn't start, so I let them take mine. I hope you don't mind that we asked Marion to fill in for you at bridge. Did you get a dog?"

"No," said Miss Cooper crisply.

Mr. Netterich, who was still staring after the departed Madame Krevotsky, woke up and glanced down at his watch. "Time for my morning stroll. Anyone else? Lydia? Marion?"

Marion said that she had to pry her husband away from his morning paper first, but promised to meet Mr. Netterich on the front drive.

"You go along, Edward," Mrs. Smith said. "It's getting rather warm out already. I think I'll wait until this evening." When they'd both left the room, she turned to Miss Cooper again. "Why don't you tell us who all your friends are, Katherine? Penny I remember, of course."

So we stood there saying "Hello" and "Nice to see you again" and smiling like we were at some fancy party. Just before she reached Mr. Harms, Mrs. Smith paused for a moment to run her fingers through her hair and wet her lips with her tongue. I'd seen girls at school go through the same ritual.

Finally everyone else left the room, and we were alone. Mrs. Smith could barely contain herself. In fact, she didn't.

"Did something else happen, Katherine?" she

asked, her eyes searching Miss Cooper's hair for tell-tale traces of twigs.

Miss Cooper sat down on one of the bridge chairs. "I believe I ate some fish."

Mrs. Smith was relieved. "And it upset your stomach!" she exclaimed. "Was it fried? I remember you ate filet of sole just last month with no trouble."

"This was more like filet of goldfish," Clinton said. "Raw," he added. It was the first time he'd spoken since we'd arrived.

"Oh, you mean sushi. The Japanese are very inventive when it comes to food, aren't they?" said Mrs. Smith. "Charles enjoyed Oriental cooking. Actually he enjoyed any sort of cooking. Which is why —"

Mr. Harms had been listening with a great deal of interest. "Goldfish? What goldfish?" he asked.

Clinton and I exchanged glances.

He caught on fast. "*My* fish?"

"I'm afraid so," admitted Miss Cooper.

"What are you, some kind of nut? That prank went out with cramming a hundred people into a phone booth."

Miss Cooper drew herself up tall. "I can assure you it was no prank, sir."

Mr. Harms turned toward Clinton. Clinton opened his mouth, but he couldn't seem to find any words.

"It wasn't his fault," I said hastily. "You see, Miss Cooper was holding the Lhasa apso —"

"What's a . . . " Lydia Smith began, then trailed off.

"She must have fallen asleep," I told Mr. Harms.

"Clinton forgot about her and locked up the Green Lizard and went home. I mean, he finally did remember, Mr. Harms, and he came and got me and we went back to the store and there were . . . uh, there were —"

"No fish," supplied Clinton. He giggled nervously. "No goldfish, no mollies, no guppies. Down the hatch, every one of them."

I was beginning to get seasick.

"All of them?" asked Mr. Harms. "Even the — the *piranhas?*"

But before I could assure him that Miss Cooper had fortunately missed the tank behind the counter, Marion, Mr. Netterich's bridge partner, burst through the door.

"Oh, Lydia!" she cried. "It's Edward. They just found him wandering around in the kitchen. He had an empty soup can in his mouth. And when the cook tried to take it away, he — he — dear me, I can hardly believe it! He just put his head down and butted her right in the stomach!"

Miss Cooper raised her eyes to heaven.

10

The hall was a forest of gray and white heads. Those closest to the action were passing along what information they could gather to those who either had come in late or were having trouble hearing.

"Who did you say it was?"

"*Ed*ward."

"*Who?*"

"What's the matter with him?"

"If he's choking, I know that Heimlich maneuver."

"They've taken him to the visitors' waiting room and closed the door."

"*Who?*"

"*Yikes!*"

That last remark was from me. Lydia Smith had gone off to see what she could find out. The rest of us were standing in the doorway waiting for her to come back when suddenly a shock tore through my body. I must have jumped a mile, and when I landed, I found myself face-to-face with Alice Pringle, the hitchhiker.

Her hair was sticking out like little wires from her head. Her eyes had a wild look to them, too.

"You must be my cleaning girl. I told Miss Bitterman, the dust that comes in here in the summer is just terrible. We don't have air-conditioning, you know. Well, if you'll come along, I'll show you what needs to be done." She made a move to grab me again.

"I'm just a visitor, Mrs. Pringle," I said quickly, edging out of reach. "Your cleaning girl will probably be here soon."

She gave a little sigh but didn't argue. Shifting most of her weight onto a thick wooden cane, she started to thread her way painfully through the crowd. She reminded me of a pinball machine, the way she kept bouncing off first one person and then the next. And every time she touched somebody, you could see the reaction. It certainly was weird. But then, what I'd consider weird almost anywhere else was beginning to seem normal at Beacon Manor.

Finally Jessica Bitterman came out and shooed everyone away. "Edward is fine," she assured them. "Ellen Butler is with him. As you may know, she's a retired nurse. There's no emergency, so you can all go back to your meals."

In a few minutes Lydia Smith returned. She looked slightly frazzled.

Miss Cooper didn't waste any time letting her know how she felt about this latest development. "I *was* beginning to give some consideration to moving here," she said. "Because of having people around. But now I'm not so sure it would do much good. No one, it seems, is immune."

(IMMUNE: *adjective*: protected from something harmful.)

Mrs. Smith wasn't even listening. She just kept shaking her head. "Poor Edward. He always had such wonderful health." She sounded like she was reading an obituary. "Ellen sent him to his room to rest, but I'm so worried, I just think I'll pop in and check on him. Would you like to come, Katherine? I know Edward was a particularly good friend of yours."

"*Is*." Miss Cooper stressed the present tense.

Mr. Harms coughed loudly. I'd almost forgotten he was there. "This place ain't exactly how I figured. I'd like to go home now," he declared.

"But you've only just arrived," Mrs. Smith objected. "We're going up to visit Edward. Why don't you join us? Then I'll call the Overholts, and if they've returned my car, I'll drive you back."

Edward Netterich's face bore signs of strain, but he let us in. Mr. Harms made his way on foot, leaving his wheelchair out in the hall. There wasn't room for all of us and it, too.

"Are you feeling better?" Mrs. Smith asked our host. "You gave us such a fright!"

"Did I? Miss Bitterman wasn't too clear about what happened."

"Oh, well, you —"

Miss Cooper shut Mrs. Smith up with a sharp glance. "Do you mean to say you don't remember, Edward?"

He shook his head. "That's what has me worried. I must have blanked out for a minute."

"How interesting," I heard Miss Cooper mutter. I thought so, too.

"Anyway," said Lydia Smith, "you seem to be all right now. At least there were people there to help you. Just think if you'd been alone!" She threw a pointed look back at Miss Cooper.

"Didn't you want to show Edward's apartment to Mr. Harms, Lydia dear?" Miss Cooper said sweetly. "Edward, this is Penny's neighbor, a Mr. Harms. He's thinking of joining the Senior Citizens' Club."

The two men shook hands. Mr. Netterich took Mr. Harms on the grand tour, which took about three seconds. The place was tiny; except for the bath and the kitchen, it was all pretty much one room. There was the main living area, which had a small couch, a leather recliner, and some other furniture. Tucked into a corner was a small stereo with a stack of records beside it. At the opposite end of the room was a round dinette table with two matching chairs. A bed with a navy-blue spread pulled neatly over it was partly visible in an alcove separated from the rest of the room by a wooden screen.

"I've seen roomier doghouses," grunted Mr. Harms.

"At this stage of my life," said Mr. Netterich, "I find

I have no desire to accumulate any more clutter. Naked I entered this world, and naked I shall hopefully leave."

I didn't dare look at Miss Cooper.

"Is there anything we can get you before we leave?" Mrs. Smith asked.

"No thanks," Mr. Netterich said. "I'm going to make myself some fresh tea and then just relax for the rest of the day." He picked up a cup and saucer from the table beside the recliner and walked with us to the door. As he reached past me to grab the doorknob, I found myself peering down into his cup. The bottom and sides were covered with tiny black leaves.

"Think you can read my future in there?" he joked.

I looked closer. It didn't seem like anything more than wet mush to me.

"Penny isn't a gypsy, Edward," Mrs. Smith said, laughing.

"There are very few real gypsies left in the world," Miss Cooper informed us. "Your family isn't from Romania, is it, Penny? I believe that's where many of them settled, after wandering into Central Europe from India."

Mr. Netterich laughed. "Always the teacher. You're better than an encyclopedia, Kitty."

"Romania," mused Lydia Smith. "Is that where Anna Krevotsky comes from? I'm always forgetting the name. Doesn't she even remind you of a gypsy, Katherine, with all those beads and peculiar clothes?"

"Can gypsies really tell fortunes?" I asked.

Miss Cooper hesitated.

"Some lady my mom plays Bingo with always gets a tingly feeling just before she wins," Clinton put in eagerly. "Maybe she's a gypsy."

"It could be," said Miss Cooper. "They do believe in such things. Supposedly a special power is handed down to the females in each generation."

Mr. Netterich snorted. "That's tommyrot, Kitty, and you know it."

As soon as Lydia Smith dropped all of us off on Tucker Street, Mr. Harms said he'd been up long enough and was ready for a nap. He was still muttering about the fish. Clinton offered to go back to the Green Lizard to feed the animals and clean up the water and stuff from around the tanks. All of a sudden he was acting so responsible it was almost sickening.

I wouldn't have minded a half-hour nap myself. I was too keyed up, though. The morning had been filled with one impossible thing after another, and none of them made any sense. I went inside and fixed myself some lunch, then just picked at my food as I stared out the window.

As I said, I'd never been around old people much, but lately I'd been making up for lost time. They — Miss Cooper, Lydia Smith, Mr. Netterich — weren't like my friends from school, and they weren't like parents, either. In a way they sort of combined the best parts of each. I enjoyed their company a lot, though I felt bad that I hadn't been of more help with their problems. It was as if some wizard had cast an evil spell on almost everyone connected with Beacon Manor.

I was still sitting there at three o'clock when my mother came in. She was wearing a sun hat and a long-sleeved T-shirt.

"Back already?" I asked, secretly glad that Bert Reynolds wasn't with her. I wasn't ready to get into *that* scene.

She tossed the beach umbrella and the cooler out the door to the garage. Then she took a deep breath and let it out again.

"Something the matter?"

"Yes. Men."

Uh-oh.

She picked up a straw bag that she'd dropped on the floor and dumped out the contents on the kitchen table. There was a mess of sand and half a dozen plastic bottles. "Look at that. I have enough sunscreen here to protect the skin of every man, woman, and child in North America for the next two hundred years. Do you think your friend Mr. Reynolds would use any?"

My friend?

"Not on your life!" she went on. "'I'm OK,' he says. 'I don't burn,' he says. Well, you ought to see your friend now! He looks like a cross between a cranberry bog and Santa Claus's nose! I think I'll call him up at about six o'clock in the morning and ask him if he's still 'OK.'"

She slammed around for a few more minutes, then let the rest of it out. "And if that wasn't bad enough, would you believe we ran out of *gas*?"

112

In the middle of the day? Dumb move, Bert.

"On some godforsaken country road with nothing but fields and cows for a mile and a half! So I had to sit in that toaster-oven of a van for nearly an hour while he went for a joyride on a tractor! *Men*," she said again.

Goodbye Bert, and back to the DateMate ads.

She stomped out, and then I heard thuds coming from the living room. She came back holding a book.

"If I ever needed this, I need it now," she said.

I looked at the cover. It was *Innerpeace*. "What are you going to do?"

"Meditate. I need to calm down. Get in touch with my real self. And then I might just hypnotize myself to forget I ever knew the jerk."

She disappeared upstairs for a few hours but came down for dinner (Hamburger Supreme again) and then sat with me through "Jeopardy," a couple of sitcoms, and about fifteen minutes of the All-American College Coed contest, which was all either of us could stay awake for.

It was hot and sticky in my room. Exhausted, I got myself ready for bed and slipped between the sheets.

But as soon as my eyes closed, my head turned into a giant stage with people parading across it. First came a green-faced Miss Cooper, and Alice Pringle, the human pinball machine. Then there was Mr. Netterich, balancing a teacup on his head. After him came Agatha Potts, using a magnifying glass as a microphone and singing a song about "It's not where you look. . . ." Clinton came next. He was wearing a gold

113

earring in one ear and doing some kind of funky dance. Then my mother showed up. Her eyes were closed, as if she was meditating, and she was followed by Bert Reynolds, who looked like a neon Budweiser sign. Finally Mr. Harms' wheelchair rolled into view, being pushed by two big goldfish. And the whole time a voice was calling from backstage: "Here, kitty. Here, kitty, kitty."

11

The digital clock on my nightstand said 9:48. My feet hit the floor. I felt refreshed, and my mind was clear. No, better than clear. While I was sleeping, the whole business about Miss Cooper had sorted itself out. I knew who, I knew how, and I knew why. At least, I was pretty sure I did. The only thing left to do was test it.

I got dressed, then spent fifteen minutes with my nose in a book. When I was satisfied that my suspicions weren't totally off-base, I called Miss Cooper and asked her to meet me at Beacon Manor as soon as she could.

"I can get a bus shortly," she said. "But why?"

I didn't want to explain. Not yet. Even though Agatha Potts was just a kid, at the end of every case she always did what any good detective did: she got everybody together in one room and solved it right in front of them. I wanted to have my moment of triumph, too.

"It's very important," I said. "It's about the tree and the fish and everything."

She didn't ask any more questions. I toasted an onion bagel and ate it standing up, licking off the butter that dripped down my fingers. Then I wrote a note for my mother so she wouldn't call out the sheriff and a posse, got my bike out of the garage, and started off.

Just as I peeled out of the driveway, Clinton De Witt came scooting along Tucker Street on a skateboard, and I nearly ran him down. I squeezed the life out of my handbrakes, just about standing the bike on end. He never even noticed.

"For cripes' sake, Clinton, you almost killed me!" I yelled.

He coasted to a stop and blinked at me. "Huh?"

"What are you doing on that thing?"

He looked down at the skateboard as if it had materialized out of thin air. "I ran over a piece of glass with my bike last night," he said. "I borrowed this from my brother so I could get to the Lizard early. I've been reading all of Mr. Harms' animal books. I'm going to be a veterinarian." He held out a copy of *All about Your Cockatiel.*

I sighed. As usual, Clinton was taking an inch and stretching it to infinity. I hoped he'd wait a day or two before he opened up his practice.

"Where are you going, Penny?" he asked.

"Beacon Manor. And I've got to hurry. I think I know why Miss Cooper ate those fish." The temptation was too great. "She was hypnotized!"

116

For a minute the old Clinton was back — the one who didn't believe girls had any brains. "You're nuts," he said.

"I don't have time to explain right now," I said, beginning to worry that I wouldn't be able to get anyone to take me seriously. "I want to get there before something else happens."

Clinton was torn. His career as Supervet was calling, but he was human, too. I think he desperately needed to see someone else screw up for a change — me. Before I'd gone fifty feet, he was pumping along after me like a dog chasing a pizza wagon. "Penny! Wait! Let me come, too!"

I slowed down and let him catch up. "OK. Grab the back of my bike! And hang on!"

I was glad I couldn't see Clinton's face during that wild ride. I tried to miss potholes and big cracks in the pavement, but some of them were pretty close calls. A couple of times I thought I'd lost him. Only the clickety-clack of his skateboard wheels told me he was still there.

In no time at all, it seemed, I was braking to a halt at the side of Beacon Manor's front porch. I didn't even give Clinton a chance to catch his breath. I grabbed his arm and pulled him up the steps.

Miss Cooper was in the lobby, chatting with Miss Bitterman. She smiled when she saw us. "Goodness, you look all out of breath."

I wiped the sweat off my forehead with the back of my hand. "Where's Mrs. Smith?" I asked. "And Mr. Netterich?"

"I believe I saw Edward heading toward the laundry a little while ago," Miss Bitterman said. "And Lydia may possibly be in her room. Did they know you were coming?"

"Penny said —" Clinton began.

"We're teaching these youngsters the essentials of bridge," put in Miss Cooper smoothly. "They're at the proper age to begin."

"That's lovely," murmured Miss Bitterman. "Well, I'll just run along, then, and leave you to it."

"Just what is going on, Penny?" asked Miss Cooper when Miss Bitterman was safely out of earshot. "I could tell that you didn't want to say anything, but —"

"I know what your problem is." I ignored Clinton's snicker. "And maybe Mr. Netterich's, too. You're not senile, and you don't have to give up your house."

"Then you've found an explanation," Miss Cooper said with relief. "I never really stopped believing there must be one."

I wondered if she'd still feel the same when she heard my theory.

We met Edward Netterich coming down the hall carrying a wicker basket piled high with folded clothes. He looked tired, as if he hadn't quite recovered from the incident of the day before. He wasn't sure why we wanted him to come to Mrs. Smith's room, but he followed along anyway, basket and all.

Lydia Smith's room was on the second floor. Miss Cooper knocked on her door. There was the sound of footsteps, then nothing.

"She's looking through the peephole," Miss Cooper said, pointing to a tiny glass bubble set in the door. "You can't be too careful when you live alone. Not even here. There's just no telling."

"Why, Katherine!" exclaimed Mrs. Smith when she'd unhooked the chain and opened the door. "We don't play bridge on Saturday, dear. Did you forget?"

"I did not," replied Miss Cooper. "Penny here seems to have an idea about why all these strange things have been happening to us."

"Not to *all* of us," said Mrs. Smith, pointedly.

"No," I admitted, "and that's really what got me thinking."

She frowned. "I don't understand."

"Why don't we make ourselves comfortable?" suggested Mr. Netterich. He set his basket down inside the kitchen.

The two ladies sat together on a small loveseat. Clinton waited until Mr. Netterich had lowered himself into a wooden rocker, then took one of the smaller chairs. I stood in the middle of the rug. With my fingers crossed.

"Mr. Netterich," I began, "It was something you said that gave me my first clue."

"Me?"

"Yes. You called Miss Cooper Kitty."

"A nickname," Miss Cooper said. "Edward is the only one who uses it."

"But didn't Madame Krevotsky also call you a she-cat?"

"In a moment of irritation, yes. It meant nothing."

"To you, maybe," I said. "Now, what are some of the things that cats do?"

"Purr," offered Lydia Smith. "Drink milk."

"And they climb trees," answered Clinton. "Like my aunt's. And yours, too, Penny."

"Exactly." Now wasn't the time to straighten him out on that.

"And they eat fi —"

"Miss Cooper," I interrupted, "I think —" I took a deep breath. "I think Madame Krevotsky hypnotized you into thinking you're a cat."

"*What?*" they all cried at once. They sounded like the Mormon Tabernacle Choir warming up.

"She's probably a gypsy," I said. "She comes from the right area, anyway. I don't know if I believe all that stuff about special powers, but I do know a little bit about hypnosis. My mom has some books on it. I read up on it this morning. It's real. People can hypnotize themselves, but they can also be hypnotized by someone else without even being aware of it. Someone can plant a suggestion in your mind and then when you hear a certain word — or see an object, maybe — you respond to it. Some doctors use it to get people to quit smoking."

"Anna Krevotsky is certainly no doctor," Miss Cooper remarked.

"You don't have to be. It's mind over matter. Miss Cooper, you and Mr. Netterich both made Madame Krevotsky mad when you were playing bridge with her. I think she's getting revenge."

Miss Cooper nodded slowly. "It could be, Edward. You've seen that pendant she wears around her neck. She's always playing with it at the bridge table. I remember staring at it one day and almost dozing off."

"Just a minute," interrupted Edward Netterich. "*You* may have been hypnotized, Kitty, if you care to believe that, but *I* certainly wasn't."

There was a sudden silence. I'd forgotten that he still didn't know what had really happened to him. I glanced at Miss Cooper.

"It wasn't your fault, Edward," said Lydia Smith gently. "You don't normally go around chewing on old cans."

"Chewing on cans?"

"'An old goat,'" murmured Miss Cooper.

"Goats eat garbage," said Clinton. Maybe he *would* make a good vet — with a little more education, of course.

"Oh no." Mr. Netterich covered his face with his hands.

"What about Alice Pringle?" Lydia Smith asked suddenly. "She's been acting funny, too, and she doesn't even play bridge."

"But she's a hitchhiker," I said. "You know yourself how annoyed everyone gets when she hooks onto them. Madame Krevotsky could have hypnotized her into giving out shocks that would keep people away from her."

"I notice she's been shuffling her feet more," said Miss Cooper. "She has probably built up static electricity from the carpet."

I didn't have anything more to say.

"Goodness!" exclaimed Lydia Smith after a short pause. "What a perfectly nasty thing to do!"

"It's also pretty farfetched." Mr. Netterich was slowly recovering from his shock. "But even if what Penny says is true — and mind you, I'm not saying I necessarily believe such idiocy — how would you suggest we stop it?"

"Confiscate the pendant," said Miss Cooper firmly.

"Do what?" asked Clinton.

"Clinton, if you're ever going to grow up to be a responsible citizen, you're going to have to listen more closely," I said, exasperated. "You can't have every single thing explained to you. Use your ears. To confiscate something means to take it away. We're simply going to take the pendant away from Madame Krevotsky. Then perhaps everyone will be back to normal."

"She might not give it to you."

Clinton may have been somewhat insecure, but just then he was also somewhat right. We couldn't just walk up and ask the woman to hand over her jewelry. She'd laugh in our faces — and then probably turn us all into a bunch of rutabagas.

"I know," said Mrs. Smith. "I'm her bridge partner. Obviously she has nothing against me, or else I'd have been swinging through the trees like a chimpanzee, too. Why don't I tell her I've been admiring the pendant and then ask to borrow it? Afterward I can always say I lost it and offer to replace it. Of course, if it's from Romania, she wouldn't expect me to fly overseas just to buy her another one."

"A very clever suggestion, Lydia," Miss Cooper said, ignoring the chimp bit.

Lydia Smith beamed.

"*Hmmm,*" said Edward Netterich thoughtfully.

Nobody could think of a better plan, so we soon found ourselves in the other wing, in front of a door with a little brass sign.

MADAME ANNA KREVOTSKY.

"We'd better stay back out of sight," suggested Miss Cooper. "Lydia will have to get inside in order to get the pendant. It might be more plausible if she were alone."

(PLAUSIBLE: *adjective*: believable.)

I was worried. Mrs. Smith was acting like this was an audition for a school play. She might get so wrapped up in playing her part that she'd forget what she was really there for.

"Let me go, too," I pleaded. Agatha Potts wouldn't have missed this for the world. Neither would I! "I could make believe I'm her granddaughter." That would be easy enough. Everyone around Beacon Manor seemed to automatically assume I was somebody's relative.

Miss Cooper understood. She nodded at Mrs. Smith. Then she, Mr. Netterich, and Clinton slipped out of sight behind a nearby corner. I noticed Mrs. Smith's hands trembling as she knocked.

For a minute nothing happened. Through the door I could hear violin music. It was so sad it almost made me want to cry. Then there was the rattle of a chain, and Madame Krevotsky's face appeared in the opening.

123

"Yessss?" If I hadn't been able to see her, I'd have thought we were talking to a snake.

"Oh, Anna," chirped Mrs. Smith. "My ... er ... granddaughter and I are going out for — for — oh, for lunch, of course. I was just wondering if I could borrow those lovely beads of yours. They always make you look so stunning."

Madame Krevotsky scowled, but she unhooked the latch and let us in.

Her apartment had the same layout as Edward Netterich's and Mrs. Smith's, but the resemblance stopped there. The furniture was all made of dark, heavy wood, with dark, heavy upholstery. Even though the windows were open, the sun wasn't shining inside. A faint odor hung in the air. It reminded me of one of those novelty shops at the mall. I stole a peek around to see if I could spot a crystal ball somewhere. With a sort of sigh, the door closed behind us.

Madame Krevotsky had disappeared. I heard drawers being pulled open and slammed shut. Then she returned. From her fingers hung the colorful beads I'd seen around her neck earlier. But not the gold pendant.

"You must know zat it is only because we play ze bridge together zo good zat I am loaning these to you," she said. "But beware! Zey are beads belonging to my mother. The woman who wear them will find romance."

"That's silly," Mrs. Smith protested with a giggle. "At my age, Anna?"

"Love has no rules. It can come to any."

I wondered if I could talk her into lending the beads to my mother for a while.

Mrs. Smith slipped the strands around her neck and turned to look at herself in an old oval mirror that hung on the wall. She fussed with them, moving them all around, back and forth. I was beginning to think my fears about her getting carried away had been justified. But finally she lowered her hands. "They just don't seem to have the same exotic look as when you wear them," she told Madame Krevotsky. "It needs a special touch. Maybe that pendant of yours."

Anna Krevotsky's eyes narrowed. "My pendant? Zat I do not loan." And she dug deep into the folds of her long skirt and pulled it out.

"Oh, please," Mrs. Smith said desperately. "Just for tonight? I'll bring it back immediately."

"No."

What were we supposed to do now? This was getting to be more than slightly ridiculous. I'd let my imagination run away with me. The pendant was only another piece of junk jewelry, like the "love beads."

But if so, I asked myself, why was Madame being so cautious about it?

"It's very beautiful, Madame," I said. "May I hold it for a minute?"

She walked up close to me and, taking my head in her hands, looked deep into my eyes. "Ah, I zee a very wise young lady inside," she said. "One who understands too much, maybe? Who is trying to fool old Krevotsky? Like a sly fox you are, eh?"

"N-n-not me," I stammered. I felt funny. And

tired — which was surprising, considering how late I'd slept that morning. My leg began itching. Absently, I reached down and scratched it.

"Yess. A nize fox. Poor, tired fox."

My whole body went limp. I had a terrible desire to lie right down there on the floor and slip off to sleep. My eyeballs were just beginning to roll upward when I realized what was happening. Madame Krevotsky was trying to hypnotize me!

"Help!" I croaked.

Through a haze, I could see the door swing slowly on its hinges. Then Clinton edged into the room. Behind him came Edward Netterich. Instead of the cavalry riding to my rescue, all I had was an old man and a young coward. The itch on my leg — like a dozen flea bites — was growing unbearable. I longed to get my fingernails on it, but I couldn't seem to move.

"Pretty, pretty fox," she crooned, stroking my forehead with long, bony fingers.

I was growing weaker and weaker. Just as my eyes were closing for the last time, however, I saw a movement. It was Miss Cooper! Her back was flat against the wall as she inched her way toward Madame and me. Please, I prayed silently.

Madame wasn't paying any attention to her. I guess she thought she had everything under control. Then, suddenly, Miss Cooper's long arm darted out and snatched the pendant away. Madame let go of me. I sank to my knees.

"Give it back!" screamed Madame.

"Certainly not, you — you —" It sounded like *witch*, only not quite.

Madame lunged.

"Catch, Edward!" Miss Cooper called, and she tossed him the pendant.

It looked like a good enough throw, but she was short by a mile. The pendant landed in the middle of the carpet.

Madame dove for it. So did somebody else. It wasn't clear right away which one of them had recovered the fumble.

"Let *go!*" Madame shrieked. "You will break it. It doess you no good. Zee? My hand still holds ze chain, and zo the pendant will do my bidding!"

I scrambled to my feet and saw Clinton clutching the other end of the gold chain.

Madame's eyes swept the room with a fierce red glow. "You are all animals," she spat.

"Naa," bleated Edward Netterich.

Miss Cooper began licking her hand.

"Oh dear," Lydia Smith gasped.

"And *you*," Madame Krevotsky turned on her. "You are ze worst. A traitor!"

As Mrs. Smith backed up, quivering in terror, Clinton yanked hard, taking Madame by surprise. The pendant came free.

Madame Krevotsky went after Clinton like a maniac. His hair stood on end, as if he'd just watched six

Fright Night Specials in a row. But he kept hold of the chain.

"Outside!" I heard Mr. Netterich call.

An eternity went by as Clinton's head turned.

Maybe some people have gypsy blood in them and never know it. You could almost see him hypnotizing himself, and in typical Clinton style, he went overboard. But it couldn't have happened at a better time. Suddenly he was no longer Clinton the Klutz, but on the mound for the Boston Red Sox. He paused for just a second, then went into his windup. His knee came up, his arm drew back, and with all the strength he could find, he fired the gleaming gold circle straight toward the open window.

Epilogue

(EPILOGUE: *noun*: a closing section of a
story providing further comment.)

There are two things I'm never going to
do ever again in my whole life. One is write a book. (I
guess that's what this has turned into.) My teachers
were probably right after all. I could never invent
something as bizarre as what actually happened at
Beacon Manor, and anyway, my fingers have a permanent cramp. It's also pretty obvious that this isn't
going to make the top of the *New York Times* best-
seller list. Or even the bottom. But I suppose it wasn't
a complete loss. I did learn a bunch of new words.
With luck I may even remember them for a month or
two.

The second thing I'm never going to do again is be
a detective. Whenever I think about how close I came
to spending the rest of my life in a foxhole (and not
the military kind), I shudder. Agatha Potts made solv-

ing mysteries seem glamorous. After this I'll know better than to believe everything I read.

But I really did figure out the mystery of the Voice from the Mendelsohns' Maple, and I feel good about that. OK, I *did* have a little assist from Clinton right at the end.

After Clinton got rid of the pendant, Madame Krevotsky carried on for a few minutes and then calmed down. I suspected she was planning to go out and find it in the grass after we left. But I'd looked out her window and pinpointed the place where it had landed, and as soon as we were outside, I picked it out of a bush and hid it in the pocket of my jeans.

"Miss Cooper didn't really turn into a cat, did she?" Clinton asked later, when we were on the way home. I was riding slowly so he could keep up on his skateboard, although he was so proud of himself for saving the day that he probably could have just flown.

I thought about that, and about my mother's sneezing the night Miss Cooper disappeared from our living room, and about Barney's trapping Miss Cooper in a corner of Mr. Harms' kitchen, and then I realized that there were some mysteries even Agatha Potts could never solve.

Last week Clinton came over and asked to borrow the pendant for a few days. When I asked him what he wanted it for, he said he was going to try an experiment with some of the animals in Mr. Harms' store. I can see it now. Clinton De Witt's Famous Marching Mice. Good luck, Clinton.

Cherie's back from Williamsburg, all tan and full of stories about this guy and that guy *ad nauseam*.

(AD NAUSEAM: *adverb* [Latin]: to the point of disgust.)

I haven't mentioned anything to Cherie yet about what went on while she was away, and I probably won't. It's going to be hard enough explaining why Clinton has taken to hanging around Tucker Street. She'd never understand. I'm not altogether sure I do, either.

Bert Reynolds survived his sunburn and is trying to stage a comeback with my mother. I guess it's too soon to tell if anything will come of it. I like the guy, myself, even though he keeps calling me Potts. At least with his job, we'd never have to worry about getting lost when we went on vacations.

The Beacon Manor Senior Citizen Residence is quiet and peaceful again. I've been back a couple of times, and I really enjoy my visits. It feels like I've inherited a whole bunch of relatives. Mr. Netterich is teaching me a card game called hearts, which is something like bridge but not quite so complicated. I usually lose, and I've been thinking about asking Madame Krevotsky for some private lessons — or maybe some magic beads.

Miss Cooper has been coming over regularly to help Mr. Harms in the Green Lizard. She brings the little Lhasa apso, whose name is — what else? — Gypsy. She and Mr. Harms still argue over practically everything. I think they enjoy it. The latest fight, Miss

Cooper told me, was about whether it made any sense for both of them to be living alone. Mr. Harms said he wasn't going to tolerate some bossy female rearranging his house, and Miss Cooper said that just because a person was physically handicapped, it didn't mean he should let his mind become stagnant.

(STAGNANT: *adjective:* not moving, dull, sluggish.)

I'm trying not to get involved. I've had more than enough excitement for one summer. But my mother thinks Mr. Harms is just being his usual grumpy self and that underneath he'd probably like it if Miss Cooper moved in with him. The problem is, she told me, he's secretly worried about what the neighbors might say. Well, I guess there's just enough Agatha Potts left in me to know that it's not so much a matter of where you look, but what you see.